Critical Praise for Nelson George's
The Plot Against Hip Hop: A D Hunter Mystery

- Finalist for the 2012 NAACP Image Award in Literature

"George is an ace at interlacing the real dramas of the world . . . the book's slim length and flyweight depth could make it an artifact of this particular zeitgeist in American history. Playas and haters and celebrity cameos fuel a novel that is wickedly entertaining while being frozen in time." **—Kirkus Reviews**

"This hard-boiled tale is jazzed up with authentic street slang and name-dropping (Biggie, Mary J. Blige, Lil Wayne, and Chuck D) . . . George's tightly packaged mystery pivots on a believable conspiracy . . . and his street cred shines in his descriptions of Harlem and Brownsville's mean streets." **—Library Journal**

"George is a well-known, respected hip-hop chronicler . . . Now he adds crime fiction to his resume with a carefully plotted crime novel peopled by believable characters and real-life hip-hop personalities." **—Booklist**

"George's prose sparkles with an effortless humanity, bringing his characters to life in a way that seems true and beautiful. The story—and the conspiracy behind it—is one we all need to hear as consumers and creators in the post-hardcore hip-hop world." **—Shelf Awareness**

"Part procedural murder mystery, part conspiracy-theory manifesto, Nelson George's *The Plot Against Hip Hop* reads like the PTSD fever dream of a renegade who's done several tours of duty in the trenches . . . *Plot's* combination of record-biz knowledge and ghetto fabulosity could have been written only by venerable music journalist Nelson George, who knows his hip-hop history . . . The writing is as New York as 'Empire State of Mind,' and D is a detective compelling enough to anchor a series." **—Time Out New York**

"A breakbeat detective story . . . George invents as much as he curates, as out-landish conspiracy theories clash with real-life figures. But what makes the book such a fascinating read is its simultaneous strict adherence to hip-hop's archetypes and tropes while candidly acknowledging the absurdity of the music's current big-business era. There's a late-capitalism logic at work here. If this book had been written in the early '90s, it would have been about the insurgent artistry of hip-hop musicians and the social-justice strides the genre was effecting. Today, it's a procedural about the death of principles." **—*Time Out Chicago***

"*The Plot Against Hip Hop* is a quick-moving murder mystery that educates its audience on Hip Hop's pioneer generation along the way . . . it is a nostalgic look at a magical and manic moment in time." **—*New York Journal of Books***

"George very masterfully has created a novel that informs as well as entertains."
—*Huffington Post*

"A welcome nostalgic trip." **—*Chicago Tribune***

"Nelson George comes from an older generation that still remembers Hip Hop as the vital and dangerous voice it once was. This feeling for the past carries through-out the novel, and manages to convey the weight and importance of this profound shift in values without being nostalgic . . . *The Plot Against Hip Hop* is a fine piece of 'edutainment'—both exciting and thought provoking . . . it's great to finally have a novel about Hip Hop written by one of [its] original documentary journalists."
—*ABORT Magazine*

"One of our coolest cultural critics has written a mystery page-turner about the underbelly of hip hop, and it's woven with signature whip-smart insights into music. Nelson George's smooth security-guard-turned-detective, a.k.a. D, scours a demimonde as glamorous as Chandler's Los Angeles. This plot has more twists and turns than a pole dancer, and D definitely needs an encore—he's destined to become a classic." **—Mary Karr, author of *The Liars' Club***

Jelena Vukotic

Nelson George is an author, filmmaker, and lifelong resident of Brooklyn. His novels include the first two in his D Hunter mystery series, *The Accidental Hunter* and *The Plot Against Hip Hop*. Among his many nonfiction works are *The Death of Rhythm & Blues*, *Hip Hop America*, and the recently published *The Hippest Trip in America: Soul Train and the Evolution of Culture & Style*. As a filmmaker he's directed the documentaries *Brooklyn Boheme* for Revolt, *The Announcement* for ESPN, and *Finding the Funk* for VH1.

The
Lost Treasures
of R&B

The Lost Treasures of R&B

a D Hunter mystery

BY NELSON GEORGE

Published by Akashic Books
©2015 Nelson George

Hardcover ISBN-13: 978-1-61775-341-1
Trade Paperback ISBN-13: 978-1-61775-316-9
Library of Congress Control Number: 2014938695

Akashic Books
info@akashicbooks.com
www.akashicbooks.com

Dedicated to the woman who taught me to read—
my mother, Arizona B. George.

Special thanks: Samson for the fight club, Alan Leeds for the access,
the UK Stunners for the fun (RIP the Queen of Clubz), and the
now departed "record men" (Joe Medlin, Jack Gibson,
Dave Clark) for embodying Edge.

I'VE GOT DREAMS TO REMEMBER

DHunter had been having sad, traumatic, musical, sometimes unspeakable, oft times prophetic dreams since he was eight. All three of his brothers had been murdered in Brownsville by then, so there was no doubt that this trauma had twisted up homeboy's subconscious.

But did these dreams really contain prophecies? He never understood them while they were happening. Not until well after the fact was their truth revealed. He certainly didn't think he deserved foresight and he sure as hell didn't want it, since it felt more an affliction than a comfort. D's dream on his last night living in Manhattan had gone like this:

A soul singer, resplendent in a shark fin–silver suit with three buttons open on his white shirt, was onstage at some Chitlin' Circuit palace that could have been Harlem's Apollo, Chicago's Regal, Philly's Uptown, or DC's Howard back when a Negro's big-city life was trapped within a few square miles per metropolis.

But the soul singer wasn't singing. From his open mouth came the percussive sounds of bass, drums, and even keyboards, as if Doug E. Fresh had been teleported back to the '60s. Break beats—"Funky Drummer," "Dance to the Drummer's Beat," "Tramp," songs recorded before D was born and reanimated by DJs and B-boys—exploded in a barrage of rhythm.

D sat alone, orchestra center, row E, seat twenty-four, his eyes locked with the shark skin–suited beat boxer as the lights went down and the singer became a living black-light poster with his teeth, cuff links, and pocket square radiating a blue neon glow.

Three female background singers appeared floating behind the singer, cooing some nonsense doo-wop sounds like street-corner kids from the '50s. Yet they were garbed in matching red Adidas sweat suits, classic white-shell toes, and the kind of red Kangols that LL used to rock. Doo-wop and hip hop, the neon blue lights, and the beats assaulted D and sent him scurrying out his seat, up the aisle, and into the lobby's blinding white light.

And then D woke up.

100 Yard Dash

Here's how it worked. A white van swung down Rockaway Avenue about seven p.m. every couple of months and scooped up a group of women waiting in the shadow of the elevated BMT subway station at Livonia Avenue. They were mostly stocky, as Brownsville women tended to be, and held their gear in shopping bags. They wore old Baby Phat sweat suits (with the long cat logo) or newer House of Deréon or Apple Bottoms jeans purchased on Pitkin Avenue, Brownsville's main shopping drag. One or two had little kids with them. A few were missing front teeth. The vets spoke to each other—recounting old fights and showing off their newest scars. A newbie or two stood off to the side eyeing the competition, wondering which of these women they'd be punching in a few hours.

In the van Deuce Chainz, the promoter of the Brooklyn B-Girl Fight Club, laid it down for first timers. Winner got three hundred dollars. Losers got fifty. Three rounds of two minutes each. Taped hands but no gloves. Mouth guards. Headgear. No biting. No spitting (unless accidental). No fighting in the van home afterward or you get kicked to the curb.

Once filled with these distaff warriors, the van rolled through a corridor of public housing, past the Tilden, Van Dyke, and Brownsville projects, scattered crumbling tenements from the twentieth century, some tracts of new local church–developed private homes, and then made a right into an industrial park of nondescript two- and three-story factories and warehouses.

The fights moved around to one of three locations in this industrial park up toward Atlantic Avenue. Except for the trainers, the audience was invitation only. Hustlers, thugs, gamblers, pimps, and other choice customers filled the room. Tims, low-slung jeans, colorful underwear, and red bandannas, both in back pockets and around necks, were in abundance. Guns were checked at the door, though Deuce Chainz's security guards wore visible holsters to let niggas know. This, after all, was the Brooklyn B-Girl Fight Club, a place as combustible as a ghetto gas oven.

Usually deserted at night save the occasional truck, on this evening the street in front of the industrial building teemed with jeeps and pedestrians, a miniparade of folks from Brownsville, East New York, and as far uptown as the Bronx's Grand Concourse. It was a bimonthly ritual in the heart of the hood that had given the world Eddie "Mustafa" Gregory, Riddick Bowe, and "Iron" Mike Tyson. Brownsville was many things, and one of them was a place where bloody knuckles reigned supreme.

Those standing outside trying to talk their way in were not surprised to see a black Denali jeep parked in front. For any ghetto celebrity, the Brooklyn B-Girl Fight Club was a requisite stop. Some thought the vehicle belonged to fight fan 50 Cent or maybe BK's de facto mayor Jay-Z. Instead, the hottest young MC in the city, Asya Roc, popped out of the jeep, china-white do-rag offset by his almond, girlish eyes and a mouthful of fronts as amber as a harvest moon.

By his side, in an oversized black tee, black jeans, and sneakers, and a woolly natural hairstyle, was D Hunter: bodyguard, student of musical history, owner of a failing security company, HIV positive, and Brownsville native son.

D never enjoyed coming to these fights (watching out-of-shape women bash for cash didn't move him), but quite a few Brooklyn MCs did, such as tonight's client. D was to go with him here and then accompany him to John F. Kennedy International Airport and put him on a flight to Europe. Asya Roc was a new breed of New York rap star who rhymed like he was from ATL or Texas. Atlanta, Memphis, and Miami ran hip hop in the twenty-first century's second decade, and if you wanted to be on the radio, even in New York, you had better put some twang in your delivery, cuz. Asya was from Canarsie, but on record he sounded like a Southern boy cruising in a candy-colored Caddy.

The bout underway featured Bloody Knuckles versus BAD, a.k.a. Bad Azz Beeyatch. Bloody Knuckles was a big gal with short dyed-blond hair and a couple of twisty tattoos on her fleshy, light-brown arms. She had no technique but swung fast and often and would definitely hurt you when she landed solid. BAD was taller but slighter, with Michael Jordan–like dark-chocolate skin, actual muscle tone, and she had some training. Her jab was very crisp and quickly she was bloodying her knuckles on Bloody Knuckles's nose. *Jab. Jab. Jab.*

Asya stood next to Junot, a Dominican fool with more diamonds in his mouth than on his glittering chain. The two were rooting for different girls just for the hell of it. Neither was invested in the fighters—as athletes, women, or even human beings.

From behind D a voice said, "You got a good heart, dude."

D turned to his right and there stood Ice, big bald head, thin salt-and-pepper line of a hair around his jawline, and drooping eyes. His burly shoulders, product of many jailhouse bench-press reps, were the size of newborn babies. The last time D had seen Ice was in the basement of a house in Canarsie a couple of years back. Also in that basement, tied to a chair, had been a rogue FBI agent (and wannabe hip hop mogul) named Eric Mayer, a nasty manipulator who'd engineered the killing of a woman dear to D along with two decades of other foul behavior. D had nodded his consent and hadn't looked back. The rogue agent hadn't been heard from and these two hadn't spoken since.

"Quiet has kept, you do too," D said back.

"In my own damn way." He gazed over at Asya Roc. "You backstopping the star over there?"

"As best I can."

"Hope you can get him out of here safe," Ice said. "A lot of people in here would like to pistol-whip him and then piss on what's left."

"I just work for him sometimes."

"Yeah. You can't be with him all the time."

"And I wouldn't want to be."

"I bet. He's why I'm here." Ice touched the backpack hanging off his left shoulder.

"This a delivery?" D asked, now worried.

Ice nodded. "All the way from one of those states where you can buy gats like Tic Tacs."

"Why are you doing it yourself?"

"Better me than one of these damn fool kids. Niggas get stupider every day. Believe that."

Over Ice's shoulder D noticed a wiry young man who, sans forty pounds and years of hard living, looked a lot like Ice. Clearly they were kin. "He with you?" D asked.

Ice didn't even turn around. "For the moment."

The young man looked uneasy and a little angry. Upon hearing Ice's comment he walked away, muttering, "I'ma go get some water."

Bloody Knuckles had absorbed the smaller woman's jabs the entire first round—kind of a ghetto rope-a-dope—and was now using her weight to bully her opponent into corners and was smacking BAD up-

5555

side the head with disrespectful vigor. It seemed just a matter of time before the smaller woman went down.

"Where is this supposed to happen?" D asked.

"Here. I know a spot in the back."

"He didn't tell me."

"Like I said, stupider every day."

BAD made a sudden comeback with a quick flurry of jabs before the round ended and, in a savvy preemptive move, raised her hands in victory despite getting pounded for most of round two.

Asya Roc told Junot he'd be right back and strutted over to where D and Ice stood. "I see you guys got acquainted and shit."

"Yeah," D said, a little irritated by the kid's tough-guy tone.

"So," the MC said, "let's do this."

Ice nodded and started past the ring with Asya behind him and D bringing up the rear. Asya Roc didn't completely owe D an explanation—it was for-hire work, after all. Show up and guard the fool. But making D part of a gun deal wasn't in his job description. This was felony shit. No plea bargain. Mandatory sentences. A gun deal transacted in the back of an illegal fight club was just plain reckless.

They went through a metal door and into a storage area converted into a dressing room where a bunch of the fighters were in various states of undress and activity. One woman was removing tape from her hand. Another was squeezing her red-tinted weave under headgear. Another was making out with a boyish little teenaged girl. They paid scant attention to the three men.

The trio entered a small washroom—toilet, stall, urinal, sink—all of it grimy. The room smelled like mildew stirred in a blender with vomit. D knew this was about the worst place imaginable for this transaction. One way in and out. No windows. No backup. D was cool with Ice—

they had a serious bond—but would Ice have set up a jack move on this sucker MC before he knew D was on the case?

Ice took the backpack off his shoulder and handed it to Asya Roc, who unzipped it greedily. Two Berettas. A Desert Eagle. A couple boxes of bullets.

"Yes," Asya Roc said. He stuck his hands in the backpack and pulled out the two Berettas and held them up like Eastwood in *Josey Wales.* Ice rolled his eyes at D.

At that moment, the door burst open and a pint-sized kid with a red bandanna covering everything but his eyes stuck out a Glock like it was shit on a stick. "Yo—"

Before he got his second word out, D slammed the door on his arm twice. The gun dropped from the kid gangsta's skinny arm, but the bullet in the chamber discharged when the weapon hit the floor and lodged itself in Ice's thigh.

"Stupid motherfucker!" Ice yelled as he fell backward into the toilet stall.

Asya Roc now had the two guns out and was trying to jimmy the safety on one of them. "I'm shooting my way out!" he shouted.

D reached over and slapped Asya Roc silly with his right hand, took the guns out of his hand with his left. He dropped them both back into the backpack, grabbed the MC by the collar, and kicked the door open. The dressing room had cleared.

"Yo, get the fuck off me!" Asya said.

"Shut up," D shot back, pushing his face near the MCs, "and live." D grabbed him around the waist, damn near picking the kid up, and peered into the main room.

If anyone out there had heard the shot they didn't show it. The next bout was underway and most eyes were on the ring. All the people who'd been in the "dressing room" had evaporated save the kissing cou-ple who were holding hands just outside the door.

"Where the others?" D asked.

The boyish one replied, "I didn't see no one else, but I do need glasses."

To Asya Roc, D said, "You stay behind me. When I say run, you haul ass."

The MC, bravado on mute, murmured, "Yeah." His eyes darted un-easily around the room.

They moved past the ring, D guarding the MC like Mom on her kid's first day of school.

Junot walked up to D. "Yeah," he said, "you better get him out of here. Niggas is talkin'."

"They're doing more than that."

"Oh, that's what that was," Junot said with a half-smile. "Thought it was outside."

"You like this clown enough to help us out?" D asked.

Junot glanced over at the MC. "You know I like his money."

"Okay," D said. "I'll make sure you get hit off." He needed another set of eyes. He wasn't sure if he trusted Junot, but in a room of treacher-ous people, one semihonest Negro was an asset.

The current fight was a furious affair, both women tossing blows with video-game vigor. Most eyes still seemed to be on the match, but D knew better. There had to be someone else. A couple of someones in fact. These kids ran in packs. That punk with the gun was on some initiation mission, no doubt about that, but there was rarely a lone gun-man in the hood. D searched for signs of imminent danger, trying to separate mere curiosity from larcenous intent.

And then they were outside. The Denali was parked right out front and the driver, a wavy-haired Dominican in his thirties, hopped out and opened the door for Asya Roc.

A cutie in black stretch pants and a brunette with a bone straight-haired weave intercepted the MC. Immediately Asya, out on the street and seemingly out of danger, started kicking it to her.

D noticed another jeep, a ragged-looking late-model Range Rover with illegally tinted front windows, parked across the street and down the block. He snatched up Asya again, tossed him into the backseat.

"What the fuck!"

"Get him out of here!" D said to the driver. "Do it right now!"

"What about you?" the driver asked.

"Just get him to JFK!" D replied before slamming the door shut.

Asya Roc rolled down his window. "What about my package?"

"I'm gonna hold it."

When the Denali pulled off, D stood looking at the beat-down Range Rover. He held the bag over his head a moment. They'd want the guns, D was certain about that. He'd taken a risk not getting in the truck, but holding onto the bag was the only way to find out for sure.

Once the Denali was out of sight, the Range Rover jerked off the curb. Then it stopped. D imagined an animated conversation underway behind the tinted windows. Not awaiting its resolution, he started down the block, away from the club and deep into Brownsville.

D walked fast but didn't run. While the guys inside the jeep decided what to do, he opened the bag and looked inside at the three guns and the boxes of shells. How many bodies were on these? How'd they get here? Up I-95 from Virginia, North Carolina, or Georgia? Maybe they came cross-country from Colorado or Texas? If his client's prints weren't on at least two of them, he would have tossed them in the trash and kept moving. D was about to reach in and start wiping them down with his shirt when a shot zipped over his head. He tucked the bag under his arm like a football and turned the corner like Adrian Peterson.

At Howard Street, D ducked into the crook of a doorway. He wished he'd run in the other direction, toward the Broadway Junction station where he could have hopped on the A, C, or J, or even to Atlantic Avenue where there was an LIRR stop. Either way would have meant people to distract these fools, places to hide, and a train to escape on. In the direction he was headed now, D could duck into the projects, a place where gunplay was a bit too typical for safety, and the elevated 3 subway, which could be an escape hatch but, because it was above ground, wasn't as easy to use for shelter. He was contemplating doubling back toward the fight club when he spied the Range Rover down at the far end of the block.

The warehouses gave way to the retail strip of Pitkin Avenue, where his mother had bought him his first Nikes, and then D zigzagged through streets of tight, low homes and tenements, and then down past the Marcus Garvey projects, low-rise public housing where he'd spent some very dangerous moments. It was where he'd first met Ice. For a moment D contemplated the man's fate—a bullet in his leg would likely cause him all kinds of trouble—but this wasn't the time to be sympathetic. After all, Ice might have set the whole thing up.

D pulled out his cell phone. His sometime employee Ray Ray didn't live far away. Just over at 315 Livonia Avenue in the same Tilden project building D had been raised in. But why get the kid involved in this mess? It was best to keep moving. Speed, not reinforcements, was needed.

Now he was on Livonia Avenue where the Marcus Garvey projects ended. He made a sharp right and headed toward the Saratoga Avenue subway stop. A 3 train grinded past him on the tracks above, moving deeper into Brooklyn. Surely a train toward the city was coming soon.

He was hurrying alongside the Betsy Head Pool, a WPA relic where, decades ago, D had almost drowned before getting scooped out of the chlorine by his brother Matty who gave him mouth-to-mouth at the pool's edge. Matty had been a bigger, better man than D knew he'd ever be. But this was no time to remember.

If he was gonna die this night, D told himself, it wasn't gonna happen on Livonia Avenue. This Brownsville street had already had its chance. But vows ring hollow when bullets blaze past your head. From behind him in the direction of Rockaway Avenue and the Tilden projects, two shots had whizzed past him.

D's lungs were burning, which was a problem, but this didn't feel nearly as pressing as the fact that his right foot, left ankle, and both knees hurt with more intensity with every stride he took. Getting shot at had made every part of his body tense up and tingle with pain.

D heard feet stomping about a block behind him. Maybe half a block. Where was the car?

Two long blocks ahead was the subway station. A dubious haven but, at twelve thirty a.m. in the hood, it was all he had. Inside Betsy Head Park he spied two kids playing one-on-one under the lights. D was contemplating calling out to them when another shot landed at his feet. A thug was trying to drive the Range Rover with his left hand while shooting through the open passenger window. A bullet bounced off a cast-iron subway support and ricocheted back at the driver, cracking the jeep's rear passenger window, forcing him to swerve into the other lane.

D dashed across the next intersection, the subway staircase only a block away now. He felt vaguely relieved. He was even beginning to smile when the door to the storefront office of AKBK Reality swung open and two men walked right into his path, one of them talking about "the time I scared Lil' Z," and D ran dead into his chest. Both went flying down toward the sidewalk.

D fell atop a 230-pound Latino with the stink of rum on his breath and knocked the wind out of him. He had on a black Nets hoodie, with a fierce-looking salt-and-pepper goatee and eyes that, even in a moment of surprise, were narrow and hard. Despite the man's unfriendly visage, for a moment D felt comfortable on his ample belly.

With the assistance of his pal, a middle-aged white man with a hot-pink complexion wearing a Yankees jacket, the guy pushed D onto the sidewalk. "What the fuck! What you doing jogging at this time of night?" the Latino asked even as he struggled to rise.

The shooter who'd been chasing D on foot—a black man in his twenties wearing a red Abercrombie hoodie, holding up his loose-fitting pants with his free hand—had just reached the corner, out of breath but not malevolence. Light brown and round-faced, with fat cheeks and a mouth made for cursing, he stormed over and pulled out a box cutter. "Gimme that backpack, motherfucker!" he shouted.

"What's going on here?" the white man in the Yankees jacket yelled.

"Mind your business, you old motherfucker!" the young man said viciously.

The Latino guy, still on the ground next to D, looked at the backpack and his eyes got real wide.

D just said, "This guy is crazy"—which actually wasn't true. Angry, embarrassed, and homicidal, yes, but this fool wasn't insane. To D's surprise, the man on the ground reached over and tried to yank the backpack away from him. Instinctively he pulled away. "What are you doing?" he demanded.

"Just give that shit to me!" the Latino yelled.

The box cutter–swinging Abercrombie wearer now swung at the straps of the backpack with his weapon. D quickly rolled away from all three men.

"You got him!? You got him!?" It was the Range Rover driver, who'd pulled up to the curb and was yelling through the passenger-side window.

"Yeah," Abercrombie replied, and then stepped toward D, box cutter low and pointed at his face.

"Hold on," the Latino man said. "You ain't got shit. I'm taking that backpack."

"Back off," warned the Abercrombie kid, "unless you want an extra smile."

"Is that right?" The Latino suddenly hopped to his feet, glanced at his friend, and nodded. Two New York Police Department badges and two guns appeared, one of them aimed at Abercrombie and the other at the driver.

"Put that thing down!" shouted the white cop. "You are all under arrest!"

On the surface this looked to be a fortuitous turn of events. D was not going to be sliced and diced in some ghetto basement for the backpack. Good news. But being interrogated and possibly incarcerated for what was inside the backpack didn't strike D as ideal. The Latino cop clearly wanted the bag. What was that about? So D kicked the Abercrombie kid in the shin.

Grabbing his leg and yelling, "Motherfucker!" the young man, despite the police firearms, swung his box cutter toward D, nicking his forearm through his black jacket.

The Latino, standing close to the swinging weapon, fired first. The Yankees jacket squeezed off a second. Abercrombie was hit by both shots.

The driver, without thinking and seemingly with no plan, fired three, four, five shots at the cops, sending blood, smoke, and angry cries into the Brownsville night. The white cop yelled in pain—a bullet had landed in his shoulder.

D rolled away and then scrambled to his feet to the crackle of police walkie-talkies, the rhythm of a hip hop track pounding from the jeep, two more shots, and voices of distress, anger, and obscenity surrounding him. This was not a good place to linger.

"Come back here!" the Latino cop yelled when D took off down the street.

D heard a Manhattan-bound pulling into the nearby station and took the steps two at a time. Blissfully, there was no clerk in the booth, MTA budget cuts having seen to that, so no one noticed D's wounds. He slid his card in the slot, pushed through the turnstile, charged up more steps, and dove into an empty car on the 3 train, breathing heavily.

It wouldn't take long for the cops to figure out he'd jumped on the train. They'd be on him in two stops at most.

Next stop was Rutland Road, the last elevated station before the subway went underground. When the train pulled in, D dashed to the front of the platform, hopped down the stairs next to the tracks, and climbed over a short fence, putting himself on the dingy side of Lincoln Terrace Park. He went over another fence, headed past some crumbling tennis courts, and found himself on Eastern Parkway, a long tree-lined boulevard that ran across the spine of Brooklyn, cutting tins through Brownsville, Crown Heights, and Prospect Heights.

D walked a few blocks west to Utica Avenue, a central location for north/south buses and an express subway. He stopped by a garbage can, was about to drop the backpack in, and then changed his mind. As long as he didn't get caught with the guns, they just might be useful later.

So D made a left and then a right, crossing Union Street, which would take him through the heart of Crown Heights' Hassidic community. It was a place of peering eyes and suspicious Jewish security teams but it felt safer to him than Eastern Parkway's wide boulevard.

As he crossed New York Avenue, D suddenly felt very tired. All his joints were throbbing—his knees, his ankles, his lower back. He was in good shape but a full-on sprint through Brownsville with contraband guns hadn't been on his itinerary.

Twenty minutes later D walked wearily up Washington Avenue back to Eastern Parkway. He moved past the Brooklyn Museum's awkward, ornate, classical/modern glass entranceway. A few cars sped by him on Eastern Parkway and D hoped he didn't look too conspicuous (or memorable). When he reached the entrance to the Brooklyn Botanic Garden he paused, put his feet together, and then counted off ten long strides, stopping before the cast-iron fence that bordered the garden and the thick, dark bushes behind them.

He bent down and squeezed the backpack through the bars and deep under some bushes. Using his cell phone as a flashlight, D made sure the bag was fully covered. Satisfied, he stood up, looked around, and continued west. His new apartment was just a few blocks away. He needed to sleep. Only after that would he turn his attention to the only question that mattered: what the fuck had just happened?

. . . Til the Cops Come Knockin'

The next day the NY1 Time Warner cable channel reported that a shoot-out between two New York City policemen and two gunmen ended in the deaths of the two criminals. The official story was that two off-duty officers were walking toward their cars at the end of their shift when they were fired upon by a man from a jeep and one on foot. The off-duty officers returned fire. The two shooters, Aaron Hall and Dalvin DeGrate, had long rap sheets for violent crimes and some association with a branch of an East New York drug gang. There was a recently opened real estate office on Livonia Avenue and police theorized that the gunmen mistook them for employees of that new company and were attempting a robbery. Apparently the owners had recently reported extortion attempts to the local precinct. There was no mention of anyone matching D's description.

D chewed on his oatmeal laced with almond butter and mulled over the news report. It was going down as a botched robbery attempt in an area known for crime. *Manhattan makes it, Brooklyn takes it* was still a mantra in some parts of BK. While D's absence from the report was a momentary relief, it created a host of new worries. That cop seemed to know something about the backpack. Unlikely, yet he had been real interested in the bag when he should have been focused on the kid with the box cutter.

It was one thing to have those now-dead fools chase him and take potshots. It was another for his role in a deadly shoot-out washed clean off the books. That Latino cop would definitely remember his face. Would someone connect the incident at the fight club to this shoot-out?

D sat back on his sofa and took stock of his life. He hadn't lived in Brooklyn for decades and certainly never expected to again after he'd left like Tony Manero in *Saturday Night Fever*, Alfred Kazin in *A Walker in the City,* and thousands of other Brooklynites who'd crossed the East River to make their mark. Brooklyn was a place of your roots but not your future, unless you planned on being a cop, crook, civil servant, or candy store owner. Brooklyn had been a place to visit, Manhattan a place to thrive.

But all that had been turned upside down. Post–9/11 Fort Greene, once a site of brownstone house parties, Spike Lee joints, and butter wavy bohemian girls, was now a leafy adjunct to Manhattan—and Clinton Hill was close behind. Do-or-die Bed-Stuy, while still having deep pockets of both black ownership and poverty, was full of white pioneers getting off the C and A trains after work.

Even in the Ville, the never-ran-and-never-will land of D's youth, there were signs of protogentrification amid the microgangs and stop-and-frisk-obsessed cops. It would be a long time before his beloved (and detested) Brownsville would see serious change, but a lot of locals saw stop-and-frisk as an urban pacification tactic, and D, who knew more about plots against black people than he'd like to, couldn't totally dismiss the paranoia. Why else would that AKBK Realty office be situated on dark, deserted Livonia Avenue?

D had looked for a place in Fort Greene and Clinton Hill, but couldn't find anything affordable. Through the manager of a rap group D got a line on a reasonable rental apartment in Prospect Heights, a relatively small patch of real estate surrounded by Bedford-Stuyvesant, Clinton Hill, Park Slope, and Crown Heights. His place was just off

Washington Avenue, a few blocks down from Eastern Parkway and three of the borough's cultural touchstones—the Brooklyn Museum, the Botanic Garden, and Prospect Park. On the northwest edge of Prospect Park, next to Flatbush, was a faux version of Paris's Arc de Triomphe that D always thought was kinda weak after seeing the real thing a few years back.

In the opposite direction, going east on Eastern Parkway, was Franklin Avenue, which used to be the gateway to Crown Heights but was now home to a mini-Williamsburg with hipster bars, artisanal restaurants, and gourmet grocery stores. These days, if you walked across Eastern Parkway going south you'd be in another world. Hunkered down on the north side of the parkway was a deeply entrenched Hassidic community, folks who hadn't left when all the other white people in that section of Brooklyn had fled and were still here now when a new wave of white folks were arriving.

The Hassidim had survived the blackout of '77, the primal racial violence that followed the killing of the black child Gavin Cato by a Jewish man driving a station wagon in '91, and various small-scale confrontations with police, hipsters, and real estate developers. Despite being perpetrators of racial profiling years before the term had been invented, D respected the Hassidim, viewing them as one of the city's renegade posses, who looked upon everyone else in the city with a wary skepticism. Vigilantism in defense of your property was, in D's eyes, not only logical but necessary. That's what life in New York City had taught him. His D Security company, though now failing, was, in his mind, a secular extension of the way the Hassidim guarded their homesteads in Crown Heights, Williamsburg, and wherever else they wore their black hats.

His new apartment had one bedroom, a bathroom with a big old deep tub, a good-size living room, and a dining area next to a narrow kitchen. A letter his mother had written to him long ago about survival and love was already hung up by the dining table. He was sitting on the blue sofa he'd brought over from his soon-to-be-closed Soho office. He'd also brought over a file cabinet and safe. From his Manhattan apartment on Seventh Avenue in the 20s, he'd moved his pots and pans, the dining room table, and sundry household items. So his new Brooklyn place was a mash-up of both his old office and home.

This prewar building had lots of marble in its lobby and two rickety elevators to serve its seven floors. It was the first time since D had fled Brownsville's Tilden projects that he was living in a building with elevators and a shared incinerator. He'd vowed back then that he would never again live in a high-rise, which this was not—but the idea of having to share an incinerator with his neighbors irked him, reminding him of countless days stuffing garbage bags down the shoot at 315 Livonia. Sometimes his neighbors wouldn't shove their bags all the way down back then, so he'd have to push on their garbage as well his family's mess, a distasteful chore that still made his teeth grind. Hopefully the folks in his new building, who were paying good money for the privilege, would be more conscientious. He knew it would take a minute to get really comfortable in his new home/office. Still, there was one looming decision to make: what to paint the walls?

D got up from his sofa and walked over to the wall behind his flat-screen TV. He sat on the floor next to three cans of black paint, two brushes, and a large bottle of Poland Spring water. In his Manhattan apartment all surfaces had been black. Even the wall plugs and light switches had been painted black by the time he moved out. The sheets on his bed were a dark sepia. Over time he'd added a variety of charcoals. But the core of his self-created cave was "as black as the ace of spades," as his mother once said dismissively.

Was that what he needed in this return to Brooklyn? He'd only been back two days and shit was jumping off. Black probably wasn't the move. At least not yet. He took a gulp of Poland Spring, clicked off the TV, took in the sun on this nice early-spring afternoon, and headed out into his new Brooklyn hood.

Welcome home, D thought as he stood there on Washington Avenue. *Welcome home*.

At that moment, two men in suits emerged from a car double parked on the street. One was big, burly, and white. The other was light brown with a porn-star mustache and an air of superiority that reeked worse than his cologne.

The white one said, "Mr. D Hunter?"

"Yes, officer," D replied as he sized up them up.

"I'm Detective Otis Mayfield and this is Detective William Robinson." They did a quick badge flip for D.

"Okay, officers," D said, noting that they didn't seem ready to arrest him.

"We'd like to talk with you," Mayfield explained. "Can we come inside?"

"Officers, I was just going to get something to eat. You can join me if you'd like."

Mayfield and Robinson seemed cool about it. Didn't come to play hardball, though D knew they would love to have been invited inside. D started walking and they flanked him, with Mayfield doing the talking.

"Welcome back to Brooklyn, Mr. Hunter."

"Strange to be back," D said. "Never thought I'd be living here again."

"Not the same place, is it?"

"Yes and no. New people. High-rise condos. The Nets. But I feel like its core hasn't changed," D said. "At least not yet."

D sat at a table at the Saint Catherine on Washington and sipped on a large chai latte. Facing him were the two detectives, with Mayfield again asking the questions.

"Yes," Mayfield said, "Brownsville is still Brownsville."

"I know." D's stomach got tight but he hoped his face hadn't. Was this about the fight club or Livonia Avenue or both?

"When was the last time you were in Brownsville, Mr. Hunter?"

D decided to start with a lie. "A few days ago. I visited a young man who works for me sometimes. Raymond Robinson. Lives at 360 Livonia Avenue. Apartment 8G with his mother Janelle."

Mayfield smiled and looked at Robinson. "That's very forthcoming, Mr. Hunter. When was your last time in Brownsville before that?"

"That was awhile ago. I'd have to see my calendar."

"If you got Gmail it would be in Google Docs." Mayfield was trying to sound helpful, D thought, but he detected a note of sarcasm in the detective's voice. D could also feel some heat radiating off Detective Robinson, but clearly he was biding his time.

"Have you ever done security work for Asya Roc?"

"I've worked for A. Roc Productions a few times and, in so doing, had to put in some time with Asya Roc."

"So," Mayfield pressed, "the answer is yes?"

"Yes."

"We have eyewitnesses who put you at an illegal boxing match in Brownsville last night. You were there working for Asya Roc."

D didn't say anything. He waited for the other shoe to drop.

"You were there, weren't you?"

"Yes," D said, "as I see you already know. Sorry I wasn't forthcoming on that. I didn't wanna get involved or involve my client."

"So what happened?" Mayfield was talking like they were friends now. "We know you're not a bad guy. A lot of people in the department and in the entertainment business vouch for you. But protecting these knuckleheads can put good people in bad positions."

In response D told a detailed but imprecise account of the evening's events. He explained that Asya had rolled to Brownsville on the way to JFK. When the rapper needed to use the restroom, some minor league gangsta types tried to stick him up. D admitted to punching one robber before pulling the entertainer out of there. The car took Asya to the airport and off he went to England. End of story.

D omitted the guns, being chased around Brownsville by two thugs, and the subsequent shoot-out. He anxiously waited for the two detectives to ask him about Livonia Avenue.

"Someone mentioned a possible gun sale," Mayfield said. He plopped a mug shot down on the table. "We suspect this guy was the salesman." It was a photo of Ice.

"I know Ice. I saw him there last night. But I didn't see any transaction of that kind. In fact, the only thing I saw Ice do was bet on a couple of fights."

Mayfield looked at him quizzically. "Wasn't he involved in some sort of altercation?"

"When we came out of the restroom there was a beef among some of the bettors. That's to be expected. If I'd had my way we would never have even gone in there. Anyway, I got Asya out of that spot as quick as I could. He'll probably write a rhyme about how he shot his way out, but believe me, I grabbed the little motherfucker by his collar and carried his ass out the door."

The two detectives laughed. This was good, D thought. But they didn't say anything about Ice getting shot. Did they know? Would they tell D if they did? Maybe Ice hadn't gone to a hospital?

"So you went with Mr. Roc to JFK?" Mayfield asked.

This was a big, dangerous lie. He knew Asya and his people wouldn't cop to buying guns in a restroom. He'd be cool on that. But Asya would have to lie for D. He'd have to rely on that young MC to protect him. The kid would have a nice negotiating chip to give the police if he needed one later—he could toss D on the gun possession charges if he had to. But if D didn't get in the car to JFK, where was he? He would have been in Brownsville during the time of the Livonia shooting, a much more serious affair. If someone showed those two cops D's photo he'd soon be answering questions in a small room alongside a lawyer.

As casually as possible D said, "No." The detectives looked at each other, trying not to act surprised. "I went back inside the fight club and caught a couple more bouts before heading home."

"Okay," Mayfield said.

D knew that JFK had cameras everywhere. They could easily go find shots of Asya Roc in the terminal sans his black-clad security guard. So he decided a small lie trumped a big one.

"My spidey sense tells me you aren't telling the whole truth, Mr. Hunter." Robinson's voice was soft, almost feminine, quite a contrast to his large body.

"Well," D said, "what makes you say that?"

"Any number of reasons. Gun possession by your rapper client could cost him serious time. And you too, if you were there and do not cooperate with us. Something to think about, Mr. Bodyguard. But if Ice was there and you ID him being there with the guns, a lot can be forgiven. A *lot*." Robinson slid his card out of jacket pocket and passed it across the table.

"Keep us in mind," Mayfield said as the two officers stood up.

Robinson added, "Welcome home, D."

D watched them walk out the door, sighed, and ordered another chai latte.

COUNTRY BOY & CITY GIRL

It was D's last day in his Soho office. Most of the furniture was gone. The conference room was already empty. The table, the walkie-talkies, their chargers, the lockers filled with blue suits and T-shirts, had already been sent to storage or sold. The room was bare save two metal chairs, a couple of ancient platinum records leaned up against a wall, and a brown box that sat at his feet. Inside were twenty blue buttons with gold *D*s shining in the middle. When D Security had record labels as clients, these buttons had graced the lapels of his many employees as a symbol of his company's professionalism. Now they sat, useless as old tokens, in a box at his feet.

The record business had been contracting since Napster introduced mass downloading at the turn of the century and had fallen off the cliff when iTunes disrupted the game a few years later. D had been forced to close D Security's Soho office to cut overhead and scale back his staff, using only the most experienced folks, as competition for even the lowest security positions at drugstore gigs had become merciless, much less high-paying corporate jobs, which multinational paramilitary groups were scooping up.

After 9/11, people really wanted security. But now there were so many off-duty cops looking for extra cash that the market was flooded with burly guys licensed to carry firearms. There was a glut of security people who themselves were financially insecure. Moreover, physical security, while useful, had become old-fashioned. Cybersecurity was where the money was. Could you detect and repel hackers? If the answer was no, you were just a big piece of meat in a suit. D barely understood his damn BlackBerry, a device that labeled him as ancient as his Earthlink address. D wasn't just getting older—something he savored considering his brothers' early deaths—but was becoming functionally obsolete.

D was fondling one of his old company buttons when Edgecombe Lenox entered his office like the ghost of rhythm & blues past. Edge (as he'd been known in music circles) was wearing a three-piece royal-blue pinstriped suit, an egg shell–colored shirt, a floppy white felt hat with a royal-blue ban, a fat periwinkle-blue tie, whisper-thin gold chains, and powder-blue, pointy-toed shoes with thin blue socks. It was an outfit Bobby "Blue" Bland would have sold his soul for. Edge's gray facial hair had largely been dyed black and shaped into a sinister goatee. He also sported two defiant primo Walt "Clyde" Frazier circa 1973 muttonchop sideburns. A gold blue-faced watch adorned his left wrist and a gold bracelet hung from his right, while his fingers were filled with an assortment of rings, including a sparkling diamond on his left pinky that was bling-bling decades before Lil Wayne was conceived.

D stood up, gazed at this vision of blaxploitation glamour, and said, "Whoa."

"Good to see you too, young blood."

Edge's grip was firm, though his fingers were bony and flesh loose. Seventy-five was D's best guess of his age.

"When you said you were coming downtown to see me I was surprised, but damn, Edge, I wasn't expecting this."

"Life is long, young blood," Edge said, smiling. There were several teeth missing but the man's mouth hung proudly open. "Until they toss that dirt on, things just keep on happening."

D had last seen Edge about two years earlier at the Bronx nursing home that had been the man's residence for a decade. D had been looking into the murder of his mentor, the music historian Dwayne Robinson, and a possible conspiracy to destroy and/or control hip hop. Edge had provided no material insight into Dwayne's sad death, but the elder had related tales of paranoid government programs and deadly federal directives that lingered in the younger man's mind and, to some degree, proved prophetic about the plot against hip hop. Today's talk was not to be about black blood spilled or anti–civil rights espionage, however, but of music lost that D never knew existed.

"I got a call from London about a month ago," Edge began, his voice grainy as a dusty LP. "It was from a record collector I knew back when I was still an executive. The man would pay me two or three thousand dollars for acetates of records we'd released. It was, of course, against label policy, but dude was one of those passionate British soul music fans—the kind of guy who knew the order number of singles from the '50s and who played second guitar on records made forty years ago in a Mississippi outhouse. So I hit him off every now and then and he warmed my pocket. I'd lost contact with him when I got downsized by Sony. Figured I'd never hear from him again. Thought he was downloading music from old-school sites in whatever cave he lived in in Liverpool or Leeds or one of them pale towns in England. Then he called me up at the center. Said he wanted my help finding the rarest soul record ever made."

"And that would that be . . . ?"

"Well, I'd heard tell of it. I'm not sure it really happened, that it really existed," Edge said. "Seemed like a tall tale told by two niggas in a bar. But niggas don't always lie."

"Sounds like a good story coming. If I had some bourbon I'd pour it, my man. But as you see, I'm all packed up including the complimentary booze."

"You youngsters just don't have any sense of hospitality," Edge said, shaking his head. "Anyway, the record is called 'Country Boy & City Girl.' That was the A-side. On the B-side was an instrumental jam called 'Detroit/Memphis.'"

"Who were the artists?"

"Country Boy and City Girl."

"Country Boy and City Girl?"

"Otis Redding and Diana Ross."

"What? That's a crazy combo."

"Yeah, so the story goes that in the summer of '66, the Stax/Volt Revue played the Fox Theatre in downtown Detroit. Sam and Dave. Carla Thomas. Booker T. & the MGs. Otis was the headliner. So a lot of the Funk Brothers—"

"The Motown session cats?"

"Yes, James Jamerson, Earl Van Dyke, and all those guys who cut for Motown went to the Fox gig. Now, because the Stax guys were Memphis born and bred, the Detroit cats didn't know them but had great admiration for their playing. The Detroit cats were mostly jazz trained. Very sophisticated players cause Detroit was a serious jazz town in the '40s and '50s. Black folks had jobs up there and supported that good music. The Memphis players, mostly youngsters, weren't as musically versed as the Detroit guys, but them country niggers and crackers locked into a groove like a motherfucker.

"After the second show of the night, the Funk Brothers and the MGs hung out, cracked open some bottles, and traded stories. I mean the Detroiters were actually a little jealous of the Memphis musicians cause they got to have a band name—the MGs, the Bar-Kays, and what have you—and the Funk Brothers had no publicity, no press pictures, no photos. The only people who knew they were called the Funk Brothers were folks around Motown. Different companies, different dynamics—you know?

"First everyone went over to the Hotel Pontchartrain and hung at the bar there. Some other Detroit people came over. Marvin Gaye, who drummed some, really wanted to meet Al Jackson, the drummer of the MGs. And it was Marvin's idea that everyone go over to Hitsville on West Grand and jam. Some of the Funk Brothers thought Berry Gordy and the management wouldn't like that. Besides, that night they were supposed to be cutting tracks for Little Stevie Wonder. But Marvin knew Berry and the other higher-ups were in Hollywood negotiating a deal for a TV special, so the henhouse was unguarded.

"Once Marvin rolled off to Hitsville with Al Jackson and fine-ass Tammi Terrell, a convoy of cars followed them over. Harvey Fuqua was running the session and Stevie, who shouldn't even have been up, was laying down harmonica when Marvin and Al barged in followed by the MGs and the Funk Brothers.

"Guitars got pulled from cases. A second trap drum was set up. Bourbon and Black Label got poured into paper cups. A local business-man provided reefer. Stevie's session got hijacked. My British friend says it was Al Jackson and Benny Benjamin on drums, Jamerson on bass, Steve Cropper and a bunch of guys on guitars, Earl Van Dyke on piano, Booker T. on organ, Little Stevie on harp, Marvin, Tammi, and Otis wailing on vocals."

"Whoa, that's a damn soul all-star team," D said.

"Hell yeah, but it gets better. The Supremes had just got in that night from a gig in Philly. Diana Ross had her driver stop by the studio to pick up lyric sheets for a session the next day. So La Ross sees Carla

Thomas sipping a can of Coke on the Hitsville steps and chatting with Gladys Knight, so she knew something was up.

"She goes down into the studio and sees this incredible Motown-meets-Memphis scene, and at the center of it she sees Otis, a big, husky country boy. Not necessarily her type, but the man had sex appeal. Between Harvey, Marvin, and Otis, the idea for something like 'Tramp' is concocted and, after playing coy for a while, Ross agrees to participate. The combined band bashes it out a couple of times with Otis laughing his way through it and Diana enjoying it too.

"Now, Motown being Motown, somebody calls Berry Gordy out on the coast and drops a dime. Berry doesn't make them stop the session, but orders the engineer to embargo the tapes. So after the fun is over, the Stax musicians head back to their hotel. They have a show at the Regal in Chicago the next night and need some sleep before hitting the road. But Otis and Cropper, who are savvy about songwriting and publishing, hang around cause they want a copy of the tapes.

"Harvey Fuqua is now in a tough spot. The engineer has told them Berry's edict and he wants to follow orders. But he feels they should have a copy. So he calls Berry and Berry tells Harvey to put Otis on the phone."

"Shit," D said, "that must have been one interesting phone call."

"Hell yeah. No one really knows what was said. Harvey told people later that Otis laughed a lot and wrote something on a piece of paper. After Otis hung up he pulled Cropper aside, whispered something, and they left."

"I assume the tapes never surfaced?"

"Somehow ten copies got pressed up on the Soul label—Berry had been smart enough to actually copyright the word *soul*—so the copies were on that label," Edge explained. "It was where Berry put out records like Shorty Long's 'Function at the Junction' and shit that didn't fit the Motown formula. Somebody with a sense of humor up in Detroit put the words *Country Boy & City Girl* on the label. So there was some conversation about putting the record out, but I guess the lawyers between the two labels couldn't reach an agreement. Besides, end of the day, I'm sure the Motown people didn't think it was the right fit for the Queen of Pop."

"This was 1966? She hadn't left the Supremes yet, huh?" D said.

"She broke out in 1970."

"They had big plans for her."

"Yup. And Otis didn't have his pop hit until 'Dock of the Bay' after he died in a plane crash. So, inside Motown and the world of R&B, that record became a collector's item, then a footnote, and then a rumor."

"So you're looking for a copy?" D asked.

"And now so are you." Edge reached into his pinstriped suit and pulled out a stack of euros that he handed to D. "That's the equivalent of $5,000 American dollars."

"Why me?"

"Cause you know a lot of people and you were close to Dwayne Robinson, who knew the history. He actually mentions the record in his footnotes in *The Relentless Beat*."

"Dwayne is dead," D said softly, "and wrote that book a long time ago."

"I'm told there's another 10K in it for you."

"Who is this guy?"

"Made money in the '90s doing something with computers. R&B is his passion. He wants to complete his collection. I also think there's some kind of competition involved, but I'm hazy on the details."

"Okay. As you can see, I need the money. This millionaire British soul fan give you any clues? Also, does he have a name?"

"No name. Cool?"

"Cool."

"Some people say there might be a copy buried under the Apollo Theater."

"Shit," D said, "that would be a hell of a place to dig."

Inner City Blues

D was riding the C train across Brooklyn, an experience that brought him back to his childhood in Brownsville and reminded him how many of his friends had gone wrong. For them it hadn't been about food, shelter, and clothing, it had been about diamonds, brands, and ghetto-fab. They wanted to be envied. They wanted to be sweated and jocked and talked about. Green-tinted paper was the ticket. So D resented money because it had played him and everyone else he knew for a fool. But how else did Americans keep score?

When D was a kid he thought a lot about this on the subway whenever it got crowded. He'd look at all the people around him, crushed against each other, breathing into each other's faces, trying not to look into each other's eyes. What the fuck was this all about? Money, of course. And judging by all the Bibles, *Watchtowers*, and Korans D saw people hunched over and moving their mouths to read, religion was a damn good business.

It was about fucking too. There were babies everywhere, usually pushed by young girls who seemed either too ill-tempered or casual in their caregiving duties.

D had been one of those crying subway babies. His mother had one of those too-loud, high-pitched black girl voices that cut through the rumble of steel wheels. He had been the fourth of four boys. The murders of his three older brothers had beaten his mother down. His father? Long gone. She'd remade her life and was living down South with her devout new husband, seeking spiritual salvation in the rituals of domesticity she'd been denied as a younger woman.

A gang of black and white people got off the C train at Nostrand but D kept standing. When he was thirteen the C train was his domain. He and his boys would roll on it after school to vic niggas, scare old men, and hover over smaller kids, standing right on top of them until they damn near volunteered their train pass. For that whole silly summer of thirteen, D felt he owned this subway—the iron horse was his personal ride, and he could decide if those around him rode in fear or comfort.

D had escaped incarceration by sheer dumb luck and the influence of a cop named Tyrone "Fly Ty" Williams, the patron saint of the Hunter family who'd recently retired from the NYPD (and was now chillin' somewhere outside ATL). Like a lot of kids who'd mugged people as a teenager, D never saw himself as a criminal or thug or predator, justifying everything he'd done as an adventure. If he'd grown up in a place with fast cars and open roads, D would have been racing near cliffs on precarious curves.

At thirteen he'd wanted a thrill and robbing people had been that. Despite his size, D was never solely the muscle. He'd been a tactician. A strategist. He pointed people out, whistled that a mark was coming. He had kicked people and scared people and enjoyed the chase. These days D was all about security, keeping people safe and being a paragon of some loose virtue. He stayed as clean as hand towels, yet was always vaguely worried his bad adolescent deeds would somehow catch up with him.

D's move back to Brooklyn was triggering many unwelcome memories. But the "new" Brooklyn of today pulled him back to now. Where had all these white people come from? He remembered when they all got off at the Lafayette stop. Then some went one stop farther to Clinton-Washington. Now they went to Nostrand and sometimes all the way out to Ralph. That lots of white people, mostly in their twenties and often dressed corny, rode this far into Bed-Stuy bugged him out. Word was these new white folks had already staked claim to Bushwick, and were edging into the border of the rugged, distant ghetto hoods of Brownsville and East New York.

D was even more shocked by the goatee-growing, Converse sneaker–wearing, tight jean and peacoat–sporting black folks these hipster types rolled with. He'd dealt with more than his share of bourgie, suit-and-tie fly Negroes in his day and way too many bureaucratic Queens home-owning black people staring at him across desks at clinics, Social Security offices, and police precincts. None of them seemed that different from D except they had a nine-to-five and he didn't.

But these new black folks were from a planet D hadn't visited. So when one of these kinky-haired, peacoat-wearing dudes approached him, D didn't know what to think. In another era this guy would have been a mark, someone he and his crew of thirteen-year-olds would have smacked and jacked. The dude reached into his pocket, pulled out a flyer, and said, "You look like a music head. If you have any vinyl to sell, come through." D nodded and took the flyer as the kid and his white buddy exited the C train at Ralph. The flyer read, *VINYL DUNGEON. Bushwick.*

D surveyed it, stuffed it in his pocket, then shook his head.

THAT'S THE WAY OF THE WORLD

Rajan, fourteen years old and angry, sat on a Mother Gaston Boulevard curb holding his left leg as blood oozed out of a small gunshot wound through his jeans. He was already a vision of scarlet with his red flat-brimmed New York Yankees cap with the reflective sticker still attached, red bandanna, red hoodie, and neon-red sneakers now dotted with his own blood. His small-caliber pistol lay in the gutter next to one of his sneakers. The air stank of burnt fabric.

A kid named Z-Bo, dressed in a similar crimson costume, stood laughing. He pointed at Rajan and said, "I told you, yo, that safety wasn't on."

"Fuck you!" Rajan snapped. He was trying to seem hard but tears were welling in his eyes.

D walked over and stood there as Z-Bo used his cell phone to snap shots of his friend's predicament. "You wanna bleed to death?" D asked.

"Do I look stupid?" replied Rajan.

"Wrong answer," said D.

"Fuck you."

D reached down, grabbed the hand Rajan had shot himself with, and pressed it onto the wound. Rajan yelped but D looked him in the eye and the kid fell silent. D took Rajan's hat off, pulled off his bandanna and stretched it out, then wrapped it tight around the kid's leg. "You Damu's brother?"

"No," Rajan answered, apparently more concerned about this question than his accidently shot leg. "He my uncle."

"I don't know how you're gonna keep this from him," D said. "But maybe your boy shouldn't be posting pictures on Facebook."

Rajan turned toward Z-Bo. "You posting?"

"No," Z-Bo lied.

"Why don't you call 911?" D said.

"What?" Z-Bo said.

"Yo," D countered, "man up."

"What you sayin'?" Z-Bo said.

"Call 911, fool!" Rajan shouted.

D held out his hand. "I should take the gun."

"I paid eight hundred dollars for that gun," Rajan said. "Who the fuck are you?"

"I know your family. My name is D Hunter. I know possessing that gun will get you in more trouble than getting shot with it."

"He's right, yo," Z-Bo affirmed.

"Whatcha know anyway?" said Rajan.

A small crowd was gathering on the sidewalk now that it was clear that this gun shot was, on this day, a singular event.

D took Rajan's gun and put it in his waist against the small of his back.

"I should take the gun," Z-Bo said. D ignored him, as did Rajan.

D asked Rajan, "Your mom's at work?"

"I guess . . . No, she home."

"So you better call her."

"No. She can't see me in the gutter like this."

D said, "Bet she gets here faster than EMS," then looked at Z-Bo. "Stop taking pictures and call his moms."

Z-Bo called, pulling Rajan's mother away from the Kardashians' latest drama. Rajan was getting dizzy, but the bleeding had slowed and he was moaning through the pain, which to D suggested the kid would live. D wondered if there was a reality competition show in guessing who could get to an injured ghetto child faster—NYPD, EMS, or a reality show–watching mother.

There was some blood on D's right palm, most of it already dry. He hadn't thought about why he'd walked over to help this stupid kid. Hadn't he learned long ago that minding your business was the safest way to get through your day in Brownsville? But Rajan's uncle, Damu, had done some security work when business was good and was now in the army stationed somewhere in the Middle East.

Now here D was with a bloody hand holding the pistol of a kid who'd shot himself in the leg. Rajan was lucky as hell that he hadn't shot his own dick off. D glanced over at the onlookers and had a sobering thought: *What if this kid has hep B or even C?*

"Here comes your ma!" Z-Bo pointed down the block where an anxious heavyset black woman who looked to be in her early forties, in a shiny black-and-red bob and a pink sweat suit, was run-walking in their direction.

"You be good," D said.

"You ain't waiting?" Rajan asked.

"What for?" D said, and walked away.

Three blocks later he bent down and dropped the gun in a sewer. Then he pulled himself together and walked through the front door of Brooklyn Funeral Home & Cremation Services.

ASCENSION

D knew this place too well. All three of his brothers had had their services here, where their bloody bodies had been made presentable to the public. It was where he first encountered the news media when someone had tipped off the *New York Times* about a family with four boys, three of whom had been shot dead on the same Brooklyn street corner. A white man with a notepad had spoken to his mother and she'd given him Polaroids of her dead sons. It had all happened here in an office in the back.

Today he was a witness to someone else's pain. He sat in the back as the wake began for Dalvin DeGrate, the Abercrombie kid who'd tried to slice him with a box cutter a few days ago. D didn't really know what he'd learn at the twenty-two-year-old's wake, but there was a lot about that night he didn't understand and maybe he'd get some kind of insight into why the kid had chased him for a bagful of guns.

Mr. Elvin DeGrate had come up to Brooklyn from North Carolina as a young man, took a job with the Transit Authority, and now owned a home in East New York. In front of Dalvin's body Mr. DeGrate talked of his son's passion for football and how talented he had been as a high school wide receiver/defensive back, how dedicated he could be when given a task. Mr. DeGrate held himself erect and with great dignity even when he cried and had to be led back to his seat by a coworker.

Dalvin's little brother DeVante, sixteen and lean as a New York streetlight, reminisced about his brother showing him the ins and outs of *Madden NFL* with religious fervor. A couple other speakers rose as well, friends of the family who recalled Dalvin's childhood hijinks and sporting prowess.

But it wasn't until the kid's cousin Cedric Hailey came forward—a short, dark-skinned man with jail-built shoulders and a face of nicks and scratches—that facts surrounding Dalvin's death were actually addressed.

"I know some people, even some of the people in this room—a lot of people in here—thought Dalvin was a gangsta," Hailey said, surveying the room and waiting to be challenged. "Yeah, Dalvin is dead and he had did some dirt. But, quiet as kept, Dalvin had no choice. That's right—no choice. He was under a man's thumb and they squeezed him. That night wasn't about vic'ing nobody. It wasn't a job he had to take. So they can say what they want about him on TV. But the streets know." Hailey pulled a small bottle of vodka out of his back pocket, took a swig, poured a bit on his cousin's body, and then sat back down.

There were other speakers after that but Hailey's talk pretty much shut the wake down. D had spent the last few years living with the fallout from a conspiracy theory about hip hop. He'd never paid much attention to such theories in the past (many black folks were obsessed with them) but now he gave everything he heard some bit of credence. Did his cousin really know something or was that just the vodka talking?

In Brownsville you were always being sized up—a threat, a mark, a future baby daddy or mama, a joke, or just plain corny. It was a place where danger and opportunity were often embodied in the same person. D knew better than to just run up on Cedric Hailey, who now stood outside the funeral home on Pacific Street with two do-rag–wearing homeys who looked more hardened than him. With his unfamiliar face and black suit, D rolling over to the trio to introduce himself and ask questions would just be a waste of time and, probably, a touch dangerous.

Suddenly D felt a shadow pass over the sun. The man was NBA-power-forward big and dressed very '90s—Coogi sweater, baggy FUBU jeans, regular blue Yankees cap backward, dingy, once-white Air Force 1s, and a white do-rag.

"I seen you at the fight club. Am I right?"

"If you say so."

"I do. My people call me Ride. You D, am I right?"

D didn't feel like being bothered but this guy was too big to ignore. "Yes. D Hunter."

"I also seen you with that fool youngster who shot himself. I was walking here and saw you. Am I right?"

"You are."

"I like that. I see you out here helping people."

"Glad you do, Ride. You a friend of the family?"

"Yeah, I know them. But check this—I know *your* family too. Your brother Rah. I ran with him a bit."

"I don't remember you, Ride, and I'm sure I would."

Ride laughed. "You were a kid and Rah didn't wanna bring his business around you."

D nodded and then asked, "So when did you hit the bricks?"

"Shit," Ride said, "I ain't counting days no more. I'm out. That's all I care about."

As the two men spoke, Hailey glanced over at Ride, then smiled and came over to greet him. "Nigga, I didn't know you were home." He hugged Ride, as did his two thuggish friends, all three treating him like a fallen warrior miraculously come back to life.

"Yo," Ride said, "this is D, an OG homey of mine. He's from Tilden."

"What building?" Hailey asked.

"315," D answered, which seemed to satisfy Hailey's curiosity, then added, "I liked what you had to say." D decided to see if this introduction had possibly opened a door. "I just moved back to Brooklyn and heard about what happened and thought, *New mayor, same cops.*"

"Yeah," Hailey said softly. "I shouldn't have been putting it out in the street like that, especially in front of his father. They gonna do some kind of investigating and that could only get them in trouble. You go to the police around here and you never know who you talking to. They say the devil wears red but I know that nigga likes blue too."

An older woman, one of Hailey's aunts, walked over and started chirping at him about his comments at the wake and said Dalvin's mother wanted to speak to him. Anticipating a verbal ass-whipping, Hailey excused himself and, followed by his two friends, headed back inside the funeral home.

"You leaving, D?"

"I was thinking about it. Thanks for the intro, by the way."

"I could tell you wanted to speak with Ced. I figured I could assist and then, you know, maybe you could do me a solid."

"You know anything about what he was talking about in there?"

"I just got home. Was off the streets seven years, so I ain't really current. But I could ask around if it means something to you. You a helper type. I see that. The world needs helpers. I need a helper right now."

"Okay, what's your mission, Ride?"

"You wanna come sit with me a minute? I'm seriously hungry. My treat."

"Okay, big man. Where you wanna go?"

The two men ended up at the McDonald's near the funeral home. D had a bottled water before him, while Ride displayed a prodigious appetite: two large fries, three Quarter Pounders, an extralarge Coke, and an apple turnover for dessert.

"I need to find my woman. Her name's Eve. It's been seven years, but I love her like it was the night we met."

"What exactly did you do, Ride?"

"I hit someone. A few times. They said it was assault. I'm back. But things done changed."

"Don't you have any friends who know her and where she is now?"

"I thought I had homeys but it turned out I didn't," Ride said.

He had been the muscle for Tim Tim Mosley, a salty Jamaican with a connect in Miami and a taste for rocking Clarks Wallabees back when selling crack was wack (and extremely lucrative). Tim Tim was a character. If he wore brown Clarks the laces would be red, or if the pair were black the laces were blue. Ride met him one afternoon at a basketball tournament at the Tilden projects. Ride had once been a promising high school athlete, but too much McDonald's and a bad left knee cost him a career.

At six seven and three hundred pounds, he was too wide to run fast and had fucked up his knee in high school, so he had very little lateral mobility. But he dominated the paint that day and caught Tim Tim's eye. Ride became, no surprise here, Tim Tim's intimidator, a man so awesome in size and solemn of face that he squashed beef just by breathing. Ride claimed not to have killed anyone (that he knew of) but did breezily admit to bruising scores of people with a baseball bat (thirty-eight ounces was his preference) and, often, with his bare hands.

He'd been infatuated with Eve since they were in elementary school but Ride didn't win her love until he joined Tim Tim's posse and was clocking major figures. To launder his cash Tim Tim funded a music production company and, at Ride's urging, recruited her into a new jack swing–era group called Money Gripp that tried to be SWV and ended not as good as Total.

Ride began to suspect that Tim Tim wanted his girl (and there was evidence that the desire went both ways). Things took a nasty turn when, coming into the studio one night, Ride caught Tim Tim trying to steal a kiss. So Ride tossed Tim Tim up against the control room glass and beat him with a mic stand; only Eve's cries kept him from committing homicide.

A week later Ride was walking by the old fish market on Belmont Avenue when two patrol cars came up on the sidewalk and arrested him for assault on a rival dealer. Turned out the key piece of evidence was a bloody Louisville Slugger provided by Tim Tim.

While Ride was upstate, Tim Tim was shot dead in a drive-by while purchasing gold chains on Pitkin Avenue. One day Eve went into Manhattan to see the latest Tyler Perry play at the Beacon Theatre and never came back. She left Brownsville and Brooklyn, but not Ride's dreams on lonely, incarcerated nights.

D was trying to concentrate on Ride's story but he kept noting this very nervous-looking light-skinned brother—late twenties, red Yankees cap, gray hoodie—watching them, even as he ate fries with one hand and texted with the other.

"No worries, yo," Ride said after D gestured toward the kid. "He's not concerned with you, so don't you be concerned with him."

"You owe people something?" D asked.

"No, but a lot of people owe me. And they will repay me. But that's not your problem. Find Eve for me."

Ride pulled out a knot of bills and D was unsuccessful in concealing his sudden greed. "Relax, my dude," Ride said, smiling. "It's mostly fives and tens. But I like it when people get that look. It's fifteen hundred. Can you start with that?"

Ride stuffed the money into D's right hand under the table. The pressure from the man's fingers, thick as ballpark hot dogs, caused D to wince.

"Sorry, yo. Eve always used to say I should handle people like eggs cause if I get too angry I could hurt people." Ride reached into his wallet, which was made of reddish cloth and held together by black Velcro tabs, and out of it fell a wrinkled photo of two people surrounded by a computer-generated heart. A younger, happier Ride sat with a honey-colored cutie, blessed with a sensuous mouth and inviting bright eyes. She looked barely legal but Ride, around thirty in the photo, clearly hadn't cared.

"Is this your only picture of her?"

"That's what I can give you, yes." Ride reluctantly passed it across the table.

"Did you hurt her?"

A storm of anger passed across Ride's face and D wondered if his new employer was going to reach over the table and squeeze his head into an omelet. The skies stayed overcast but no rain fell. "I know my own strength," Ride said simply.

D pressed no further. He took the wad of bills and straightened them out, sorting them in order of denomination (fives, tens, twenties). It was a habit—it irritated the hell out of him to have disorganized money in his wallet.

"Just meet me back at this McDonald's in three days with some info on Eve. Okay, yo?"

"And if I don't have any info?"

"Make an effort for me and I will make an effort for you."

Ride stood up, leaned over, gave D a light embrace, picked up his food wrappers, dumped them in the garbage bin, and lumbered out. The light-skinned kid lingered a beat and then was out the door, moving quietly in Ride's wake.

That's not a lot of money, D mused, but it beat a blank. Now, how does one find a lost ghetto girlfriend in the twenty-first century?

I'll Always Love My Mama

Wherever poor people live today—be it a rural African village, a Brazilian favela, or an inner-city American hood—the World Wide Web is a magic carpet of interaction with the larger world. For most of Brownsville's history it was a scrappy block of land far from Sri Lanka and Soweto. Now it was all just a click away. Alas, this connectivity didn't always result in shared values.

"I be looking at these girls," Ray Ray said, "and they be mad skinny, D."

"That's true," D chuckled.

Ray Ray sat at his mother's kitchen table tapping on an Apple computer, looking at images on the Russell Simmons–owned Global Grind, a site that mixed celebrity gossip, swimsuit galleries, and political/social commentary. He and D were supposed to be using Google, Facebook, and Twitter in search of Ride's lost Eve. D didn't think he'd find this girl via the Internet but Ray Ray wanted to try and it gave D a chance to get into what he really wanted to talk about.

"I don't understand," Ray Ray said. "I see fat-ass girls on Dumont Avenue hotter than every girl on here. I mean they got some nice faces and shit, but they ain't really bringin' it like a bad bitch should."

D smiled. "You don't see Brownsville booty everywhere, Ray Ray. Russell Simmons and a lot of folks in the media world have a different standard of beauty that's got nothing to do with life in the real world. The values there are as bad as anything you'll find in the projects."

Pausing and changing his tone, D continued: "I need you to do me a solid. I was handling security for Asya Roc and he—"

"Yo, I heard about that shit," Ray Ray interrupted excitedly. "There was some shooting at the fight club. Same night there was that crazy shoot-out down by the Saratoga subway. Two niggas got murked by the cops." The young man's eyes lit up. "You were at both, weren't you?"

"Ray Ray, all you need to know, if you are ever asked, is that I came by here a few weeks back to check up on you. You don't worry about remembering the date. We talked about getting you more work and we played some video games. Plus, I didn't see your mother. It was just you and me."

"Gotcha."

"Thanks. So I'll pay you for helping me finding this Eve and, if anyone asks, that's what you've been doing for me."

"Of course."

The apartment door opened and Janelle, Ray Ray's mother, entered wearing black ankle-high boots, formfitting jeggings, a leather jacket, a burgundy blouse, a hot-pink scarf, dangling earrings that matched the scarf, and a short Halle Berry–ish weave decorated with two streaks of pink. Janelle was two shades darker than her son (a reflection of the caramel complexion of the kid's father) and had a beautifully sculpted face (full lips, sharp cheekbones), though her eyes always looked skeptical, even when laughing. Those lovely lips poked out in a perpetual pout.

"Well hello, stranger," she said to D, and gave him a long hug and a kiss on the cheek before acknowledging her son. "Boy, you know that Facebook is gonna stunt your growth. I think it already has." This was typical of Janelle—everything had stunted her slender son's growth, from video games to hip hop to Facebook. She had a habit of speaking on subjects before she really knew what was going on. "You about to work for D again?"

"Yes. I'm helping him do some research."

Janelle noticed the heart-shaped photo of Ride and Eve on the kitchen table and picked it up.

"You know her, Ma?"

"I used to see her around but heard more about her that I actually saw."

"Did you know Ride as well?"

"That big gorilla-ass motherfucker? Yeah. Nigga tried to talk to me once, but a Big Mac is no kinda date."

"So," D said, "Ride is out and looking for her. There's money in it for you and your son if you can help me find her."

"Well, she's long gone from around here. Ain't been around here since Skippy was a pup. You know, D, I don't like my boy hanging with these damn convicts out here. They like incarceration recruiters. Spend enough time with them and you will find your ass in jail."

"Janelle, I'll be the one dealing with him," he said reassuringly.

She turned to her son. "How much is D paying you?"

D had prepared three hundred dollars to give to Ray Ray for his research/cooperation but now figured he'd have to give Janelle his money and then slip the kid some cash separately. Either way, Mama was gonna get a taste, so he put the cash down on the table.

"It's *my* money, Ma."

"Okay. So that means you are only gonna spend that money on yourself and not pay no bills?"

"Ma, you know if I have, you have."

"Well, now we have three hundred dollars. You are being awfully generous, handsome," she said to D. "Ride must have given you a G or something."

"Your son and you will be compensated for whatever help you can give me. I would never jerk you two."

"Hmmm," Janelle said, "sometimes you are sillier than a bag of dust. What, you tryin' to find her on Facebook or one of them sites? She's probably using a nickname and got a blond weave and gained twenty pounds . . . Tell you what. You guarantee us another four hundred of what Ride pays you and I'll show you how to find her."

"Why does everything have to be a negotiation with you, Ma?"

"Cause I'm trying to teach you, Ray Ray. You didn't learn shit in school so I'm supplementing that bad-ass education you got."

"Okay, Ma."

"Your mama is a resource," Janelle said. "Forget Facebook. *I'm* Facebook."

"Ghetto Facebook, huh?" D said.

"Why it got to be ghetto?" Janelle asked.

"It is what it is, Ma," Ray Ray said, and both he and D laughed.

"Boy, I oughta pop you."

"So, Janelle," D asked, "do you know something or are you just messing with me?"

She held out her hand and D dug into his pocket, peeled off another hundred, and handed it to her.

"Okay, go over to Womack & Womack's over on Livonia off Saratoga. That girl Eve's sister works there. Eryka. Looks like her but rounder. She does a mean wash-and-curl though."

"Damn, Ma."

"Don't sleep on your mama, son. Now," she said, turning to D, "you staying for dinner?"

You Got Me

Even in the daytime, Livonia Avenue between the subway stops at Rockaway and Saratoga was shadowy, as any sunlight had to cut through spaces in the elevated tracks. Aside from the Marcus Garvey public housing development and Betsy Head Park, most of these blocks were either empty lots or poorly maintained buildings. Even Betsy Head, which should have flooded the street with light, felt dark because of the dust rising from its pebble-filled ball field.

"Anyone still play game here?" D asked Ray Ray as they walked past.

"A peewee football team practices here," he reported, "but their league banned games because of all the rocks. Only hard-core Ricans and Dominicans play softball on it. A bad hop out there will bust your lip."

The only respectable structure on Livonia seemed to be the renovated building near Saratoga that housed AKBK Realty and next door Womack & Womack's Hair Heaven. The real estate entity had evidently paid for some sandblasting and the installation of security lights.

D and Ray Ray were about to cross the street onto that block when a patrol car and an unmarked vehicle pulled up in front. The Latino detective from D's shoot-out emerged from inside AKBK Realty with a gun drawn and a walkie-talkie.

"Yo," Ray Ray said, "that's that Detective Rivera!"

"Okay," D said, "let's lay back."

The police ran into Womack & Womack's with serious intent. Women, some with their hair in half-finished weaves, scurried out. Mixed in with them were a couple of hairdressers.

"That one there is Eryka," Ray Ray said, pointing to a curvy black woman with blue threads in her bob weave.

The police came out a minute later pulling a fifty-something black man with a barrel chest and a blond Afro (wig) and shoved him into the back of the patrol car.

Eryka shouted at Detective Rivera, "This is bullshit! Bobby would never have no guns or shit like that in his shop!"

"Relax, Eryka," the Latino replied with a self-satisfied smirk. "We got a tip Bobby had guns in his shop. The tip proved right. He doesn't have a permit. He's an ex-con. He knows better. He's in serious trouble. Sorry."

Eryka sucked her teeth. "Can I at least get my bag out the damn shop?"

"Eryka, it's a crime scene."

"Stop the bullshit, Gerald. You know someone must have planted those guns."

"Well," Rivera said, "I hope it wasn't you."

"Bobby isn't into anything but hair."

The detective folded his arms and said evenly, "I'll listen to what he has to say and I'll give him a fair hearing. But you know we take illegal guns very serious in this precinct."

Eryka, quite the diva and not intimidated by the detective, countered, "I know you really care about the guns," and ice-grilled him like a G.

Rivera shook his head, smiled stiffly, and then let her back in Womack & Womack's. D and Ray Ray stood behind one of the elevated subway supports, clocking the activity.

When the cop and the hairdresser came back out, Eryka had her bag but was still steaming. Rivera went over and locked the door to AKBK Realty and then hopped into the unmarked car and sped off. Eryka stood in front of the beauty shop looking angry and lost.

"Are you okay, miss?" D stood a couple of feet from her appearing concerned.

She glanced at him a moment and said, "You motherfucking cops make me sick."

"I'm not a cop," he said. "I was just walking by and saw you. I apologize for interrupting."

"Oh, I'm sorry. You wearing black and all I just thought—"

"No," he said, "it happens all the time. Listen, I saw a little of what went down. It looked nasty and unnecessary."

"Very fucking unnecessary."

"Are you hungry?" he asked.

Eryka looked him up and down, from shoe size to shoulders, and decided to take him up on his offer. D had already sent Ray Ray home, thinking this was a job for a single man.

Ten minutes later they were having fish sandwiches and lemonade at a small spot Eryka knew. She'd spent most of the time venting about the way the cops treated people in Brownsville, with a particular emphasis on the nastiness of Gerald Rivera. Finally she asked D, "So what are you after, big man?"

"You don't think I was just walking by?"

"You ain't cracked for the pussy yet, which immediately lets me know you about business. Plus, you brought me lunch and didn't flinch. You ain't a cop unless you IA, which I would welcome, since that bastard Rivera is dirty as hell."

So D told her what he knew about Ride and his quest to find lost love. The story both amused and disappointed his listener.

"Well," she said, "that man is so strung out on that stunt it's crazy. But I doubt she's thought about him a day or night since he went away. As for finding her, well, she e-mails me from time to time. But she changes her e-mail and phone number. I bet she's in either Cali or Miami, or maybe some island. Girl loves flaunting her shit in a bikini as much as she loves singing. When she calls me next I'll tell her Ride is looking for her. That's all I can do for you pertaining to that."

"That's something. Thank you."

"So you a security guard?" she asked.

"I know it's crazy but I get paid to keep people safe."

"Hmmmm," she said, surveying his body again. "You good at it?"

"I'm as good as my clients let me be."

"Oh, it's like that. Where do you live?"

"Over in Prospect Heights."

"Fancy."

"Not really," he replied, slightly embarrassed. "I just moved back to Brooklyn and it's just what I could find."

"Well," Eryka said as she reached out and touched his hand, "good for Brooklyn."

Pour It Up

From a penthouse in the Williamsburgh Savings Bank Tower all of Brooklyn was spread out below like a miniature city with rows of homes, tiny rolling cars, and bundles of high-rises. Looking far to the east, D saw the cluster of sixteen-story public housing buildings in Brownsville where he'd grown up and far out beyond them the aircraft hangars of John F. Kennedy airport. To the south Brooklyn bumped up against the Atlantic with the ocean spread out behind Coney Island and the Verrazano-Narrows Bridge. Brooklyn didn't seem so big now.

Turning back around, D peered into the sun-drenched living room where Rihanna was striking poses. Behind the spiky-haired, bronze-skinned singer he could see the East River, three of the four bridges that spanned it, and the shoreline of Queens. The singer, quite fabulous in an Alexander McQueen gown, was claiming the horizon for herself, cavorting to her own music in a three-million-dollar penthouse in the converted bank building's peak.

This was a throwback day for D. When the record industry was poppin' he'd done security for scores of photo and video shoots. D thought he was doing a favor for a member of RiRi's regular team, though in reality it was an old pal tossing him a bone. He'd been told not to speak with Rihanna unless spoken to (not a problem), but he was allowed to watch her (happy to oblige).

When D was in college he'd fallen into security because it seemed an honest and worthwhile enterprise, something a man could feel good about doing. He wasn't a cop or a fireman or some other official protector of life and property, but he was big, determined, and quite able to handle himself.

Yet it had all gone sideways. He'd done security for hundreds of people, both the internationally known and those whose names passed the lips of few. He was realizing now that there had been little philosophy to his efforts. Nothing that guided his actions other than a singer, actor, or businessperson wanting to feel safe for the night. No matter how noble D found his work, he knew his clients were a motley crew. His efforts lacked a moral center, which was more a reflection on himself than anyone who paid him.

Just then a man who himself was morally suspect walked over to him. Eazy Stevie was the kind of person who enters your life by random circumstance and then assumes unearned intimacy. They'd met when D was doing security for an LA MC on a promotional jaunt through New York. D was having a hard time keeping up with the Cali slang of the MC and his posse when Eazy Stevie, who was working for the management team, helped smooth out a misunderstanding between D and the road manager. The trip was otherwise without incident but from then on Eazy Stevie acted like they'd bonded during wartime, calling him *cuz* and *blood* in a manner that left D cold.

How did this motherfucker keep getting jobs? Yet here he was again, up in Rihanna's mix and treating D liked they'd done a bid together.

"Yo, cuz," Eazy Stevie said, "how you doing? Looking good, dude."

"I'm well, Stevie. How are you?"

"I'm rolling with the hottest female artist in the world, so I'm pretty good. By the way, I don't know if you know this, but I recommended you for this gig."

D wanted to keep things simple so he just said, "I know."

"I hear you're looking for a copy of a record. An old obscure Mo-town joint."

"Am I?" D said, quite surprised.

"That's what I hear. Am I wrong?"

"You are wrong about a lot of things."

"So I've been told." Eazy Stevie sounded disappointed.

"But not about that," D said.

"D, I know you don't like me. I'm not sure why. I've never done anything to you. But I accept it. Anyway, about that record: I believe I can lead you to a copy."

"How do you know what I'm looking for?"

This question seemed to make Eazy Stevie quite happy. "You are not the first or only person Edge asked about finding that record. The old man knows a lot of people." He obviously wanted D to owe him a favor; the prospect made him giddy. For him a favor was currency that led to the next job, the next check.

"What do you get for helping me?"

"Just a finder's fee, nothing more. Though I should say there's find-ing and there's getting, and I could help you do that too. I believe a Mr. Kanye West either has a copy or is close to purchasing one."

"Okay," D said with a raised eyebrow, "gimme your number."

"Why don't you friend me on Facebook instead?"

"You gotta be kiddin'."

"My number game is a bit fluid right now. But you can always count on Mark Zuckerberg to bring folks together."

"You are serious, aren't you?"

"You've turned me down before," Eazy Stevie said. "Friend me to-night and we'll hook up this week."

D growled, "Okay," and then walked away.

After wrapping at the Williamsburgh Savings Bank location, the team hopped into two Denalis and a makeup trailer and headed up Flatbush Avenue toward Prospect Park. They made a left onto Eastern Parkway and drove into the Botanic Garden.

The cherry blossoms were in full bloom and Rihanna, now dressed in a Japanese kimono, posed amid the wind machine–aided falling leaves, a vision of Asian elegance D thought modest for the risqué vocalist. But after a round of shots, the kimono bottom came off, long cinnamon legs were exposed, and the poses shifted from PG-13 to R.

The spring light was fading but the photographer insisted on squeezing in another setup. With Rihanna still in the kimono, the three vehicles rolled into Prospect Park where she began prancing through a large meadow. By now the bottom of the kimono had been reduced to hot pants, and D, aided by Parks Department personnel and NYPD patrolmen, kept a growing crowd of fans, gawkers, and paparazzi at bay.

As the last shots of the day were clicked off, Easy Stevie reappeared and, grinning, strolled over to D. "RiRi wants me to ask you something." Tensing for the worst, D wondered what offense he'd committed against the pop siren. "She heard that you and Bridgette Haze had a thing when you worked for her."

Back in 2003, before Beyoncé and Katy Perry and Lady Gaga and Rihanna, a blond white-trash chick with some dance moves was pop's queen. That summer, Haze had camped in New York to record with hip hop–influenced songwriters and D became a part of her inner circle. That Haze was being stalked by a group of kidnappers, who had an insider in her camp, made for a twisty adventure that also ensnared his old friend, the now reclusive singer Night. One crazy weekend, D and Haze found themselves holed up in a Montauk beach house where some very unprofessional things happened between them.

"Tell her that's just an urban legend," D said, though there was a redness in his brown face that Easy Stevie read as a confession.

"I will do that," the amused industry hustler replied. "Get back to you on that other thing."

"Do that."

D was assigned to help the singer to her car. Though she didn't say a word, Rihanna recklessly eyeballed him, enjoying his discomfort. There was a moment, as he walked alongside her and some handlers, when D could have made some gesture of desire. A flirty comment. Maybe even just a bit of ass-kissing.

Instead he remained stone-faced and got her settled into her ride to Manhattan's Trump Soho hotel. An hour later in the hotel's lobby, Rihanna's regular bodyguard, fresh off an emergency root canal, met D in the lobby, thanked him for having his back, and arranged the paperwork to get him paid.

D was still contemplating Rihanna's flirty nonflirt when he exited the subway back in Brooklyn. While it was nice to know he still had some sex appeal, the idea that his summer with Bridgette Haze had reached Rihanna disturbed him. Was the legend of the big black bodyguard and the tiny white pop princess something passed on over drinks in Beverly Hills bars or on long tour bus rides across America? That wasn't how he wanted to be discussed. That shouldn't be his rep.

Who knows how many jobs that story had cost him? A rep as a randy bodyguard could have kept him from countless gigs and he'd never have known it. How much did this story contribute to D Security's failure? He began calculating how many female clients he'd had after that. Was that why Jay-Z stopped working with him after he got married?

D had just crossed Grand Army Plaza when a police van pulled up next to him. Three uniformed NYPD officers jumped out and walked swiftly toward him. D stopped in his tracks and quickly removed his hand from his pocket. One policeman stood behind him, one placed himself by his side, and the third, a sergeant, stood in front of him.

"Excuse us, sir," the sergeant said, "could we speak with you for a minute?"

"What's the problem, officer?"

Instead of replying, the sergeant, a slim black cop with *T. Riley* on his name plate, looked toward the van. Another officer—young, anxious as hell, light-skinned—popped out and approached cautiously.

"Is this him?" Sergeant T. Riley asked.

D glanced back at the young officer, whose name was Hall. Though he'd done nothing wrong, D was filled with a nervousness endemic to black men dealing with cops.

"What's going on, Sergeant Riley?" D asked.

"Just a minute," he said.

Patrolman Hall now turned to his superior, shaking his head before replying, "No sir, this is not him."

"Okay, sir," Riley said, "thank you for your time." Without another word the four cops walked back to the van and pulled away.

Ahh, Brooklyn, D thought, and headed toward Washington Avenue.

Sumthin' Sumthin'

D always had a love affair with music that not only nurtured his soul but, in various ways, had paid his bills too. He'd never mastered an instrument (back when NYC public schools actually taught children exotic subjects like music) and he couldn't sing (though he often lifted his voice to generate throaty sounds). Yet music was as much the through line of D's life as his bulk, the HIV virus within him, and the black clothes he wore religiously.

D's mother had loved R&B, particularly soul men like Teddy Pendergrass and more obscure performers like Adrian Dukes, whose "Green Lights" was her personal anthem. His three brothers had lived long enough to enjoy the prime years of the Time, Kurtis Blow, and Cameo circa "Word Up," though never had to endure the reign of Waka Flocka Flame, Macklemore, and other twenty-first century "talents."

But what D was encountering in Bushwick on this day was a culture of vinyl junkies more manic than anything he'd ever experienced. Unfortunately for D, the vinyl du jour was classic rock from the early '80s. Hair bands like Whitesnake and Mötley Crüe filled bin after bin, with Japanese buyers moving between the aisles holding shopping bags and pushing laundry carts filled with albums. D wandered wide-eyed through this strange world until a sixty-ish white man in a light blue Stax Records T-shirt waved him over.

"You look like an R&B man to me," the guy said.

"Not much R&B, soul, or funk in here."

"It used to be a bigger business. There was a nice sweet spot where you could sell to both young DJs, who'd buy in bulk, and the old-school collectors who were looking for specific R&B, blues, or jazz LPs. But between Serato and age, those markets have dried up. If you wanna make real money in vinyl now, you have to sell '70s or '80s rock to buyers like these guys. If the band could have been inspired *Spinal Tap*, it has value now." He shook his head.

"Well, I'm looking for something a lot older—a very obscure soul record. It's called 'Country Boy & City Girl.'"

"That's interesting."

"Yeah?"

"Yes indeed. I heard tell of it but never seen a copy myself. Suddenly it's a hot record."

"Other people asking for it?"

"Yeah. Had an inquiry just this morning asking about it," the shop owner said. "By the way, my name's Jerry Wexler, pleased to meet you."

"Who was it?" D responded, staying focused on the business at hand.

"Well, they asked me to keep their interest confidential."

"You good at keeping secrets?"

"I can be."

D reached into his wallet and fished out a fifty-dollar bill.

"He said *confidential*," Wexler said.

D pulled his wallet back out and dropped two more fifties on the counter.

The shop owner reached under the countertop and produced a card. D pulled out his cell phone and took a picture of it. It didn't have a name, just an e-mail address at DONDA, Kanye West's creative clearinghouse.

"I got another lead for you," Wexler said anxiously. So D placed another fifty on the tabletop. The man wrote a name and telephone number on the back of the DONDA card. "Feel free to use my name."

Two days later D was sitting in the Midtown Manhattan offices of Universal Records speaking to Lamont Holland, the man in charge of mining the company's massive back catalog for reissues. Though the record industry had shrunk, catalogs were still a low-cost source of revenue. When D finished relating the tale of "Country Boy and City Girl", Holland said, "I've definitely heard about this record."

"Really? You think it's in the Motown archives?"

"Maybe, but probably not under that name."

"You think it was mislabeled?" D asked.

"Mislabeled, yes, but maybe on purpose."

"Okay. Who would do that?"

"Someone who knew it was the rarest of the rare," Holland said cryptically. "You see, these collectors are a devoted bunch. I mean their self-esteem, how they see themselves, is sometimes wrapped up in what they possess, especially if it's a record no one else has and a lot of people want."

"I hear that," D said. "But why would someone go through the archives and mislabel such a rare record, especially if they could just grab it and bounce."

"You don't really understand what you're dealing with, do you?"

"Is there some secret vinyl shit you're not telling me about?"

"I'm not trying to patronize you, I'm just telling it's not as simple as you think."

"So school me."

"If Otis Redding and Diana Ross really made a record together, that's music history. I don't know that a true fan would steal it—but they might mislabel it and wait for the right moment to reveal it."

"Now you sound crazier than the people who hired me."

"It is what it is, D. Between other archivists who worked here before me and staff at our warehouses, a lot of people could have gone in there and hidden it, waiting to be the one to discover it, or, and this is gonna sound crazy, misplacing it just so it wouldn't be easily found, keeping it as a hidden gem for future generations, out of reach of collectors, people like whoever hired you."

"Okay," D said, growing irritated, "this feels like you're fucking with me. So let's cut the bullshit. Is there a copy of the record here or am I wasting my time?"

"You sure are blunt."

D stood up and leaned over the table. "I'm not moved by all this mystical record mumbo-jumbo. Do you have the record or not?"

"Straight answer: I'm not sure." Holland turned around and pulled two large black binders from a shelf. "There are so many vintage tracks in our archives that, even years after the Motown catalog was acquired, all of it hasn't been digitized or properly inventoried. If this track was the Supremes or Marvin Gaye it would be easier to find. When you first called about this record, I looked under Little Stevie Wonder and Diana Ross's solo work. Can't find a reference to it. But maybe it's under Earl Van Dyke, who cut an instrumental LP. I don't know and neither do you. These binders have lists of miscellaneous tracks from 1966 when Hitsville was really cookin'. You can sit here, search through these binders, look for a session that sounds right, write it down, and pass it on to me."

"Okay. If I find some sessions that work, how long would it take to find the actual tapes?"

"Couple of months is my guess," Holland said. "You see, all the archival material was moved to California a few years back to a more secure warehouse with temperature control and all that stuff. I'll send the numbers out there and, when they have time, they'll dig them out, hope they're not too brittle to play, and we will, hopefully, go from there." Holland stood. "See you after lunch."

Forty minutes later D was still there, combing through photocopies of handwritten and typed notes from 1966, a year when soul music thrived, Dr. King preached, and integration was the promised land. D felt lost in this past, so he was relieved when his BlackBerry buzzed. It was his old office building manager, Benito Benjamin, who he was tipping to take care of shutting down the Soho office.

"Yes, Benito. How are you, my man? Did I leave something in Soho?"

"No," Benito replied hurriedly. "Some people came looking for you today."

"Did they leave a business card?"

"No. Well, kind of. They wrote on your old office door."

"What happened?"

"There were three of them." Benito was suddenly whispering. "They were loud and caused a disturbance when they realized you no longer had an office there."

"What did they look like?"

"Hip hop. They looked like hip hop. I didn't call the police."

For that D was thankful. Journalist Dwayne Robinson had died on his office doorstep, uttering his last words while holding a bloody cassette tape. Bringing in cops would have reopened that whole sad story.

"Benito, can you take a picture of the tag on the door?"

"Tag?"

"The markings they made."

"Oh, I'm having someone erase them."

"Please take a picture and text it to me," D said, "and I promise you, Benito, they will not be back."

Ten minutes later a photo popped up on his BlackBerry that was clearly a gang sign. It looked like the Asya Roc logo but with some scrawls on the edge different from the diamonds around the MC's neck. D went over to Holland's computer, got on YouTube, and typed in *ARoc,* the name of the MC's record label, fashion line, and (reputed) gang affiliation.

Most of the videos were either promotional or live performances. Scrolling way down, he found some gang videos featuring young men (and a few women) who apparently were part of ARoc before it became a music brand. In one of them, three young fools around twenty, mouths and noses covered with red bandannas, each held up a gun for the camera, boasting about the seven bodies the weapons had murked. But then one of the masked men said, *"Each gat got two bodies on them niggas,"* which would be a total of six. So aside from their lack of remorse, this trio couldn't count. No point in waiting for these fools to find him—D decided to take the offensive.

At that moment Holland walked in, clearly unhappy to see D on his computer. "You find anything useful?" he asked.

"Who knows?" D said. "I gotta go deal with the *present* of black music. Sorry about using your computer. Enjoy the videos in your history."

On & On

The girl behind the desk at ARoc Productions was going over her Facebook page on the office laptop, while the Instagram feed on her iPhone made a pinging sound every time a BFF posted a picture. A couple of glossy celebrity rags and a copy of the *Source* lay on the white top of her Ikea desk. She was dark brown with prominent round lips and had a healthy thickness to her body that D noticed as he walked over to her desk.

"My name is D Hunter. I'm here to see Clee Davis," he said, polite as pie.

She looked at up him with small brown eyes circled with black eyeliner behind red glassless frames. "What's your name again?"

He repeated his name and said, "I don't have an appointment but I know he wants to see me."

"Okay. Take a seat, Mr. Hunter."

Fifteen minutes later, D, after being given a bottle of water and having flipped through the *Source* a couple of times, was being walked back into ARoc's offices by Lynda Creed (he'd gotten her name in casual conversation about Beyoncé's newest album). Clee Davis, early thirties, white, with brown seriously peaked hair and a shirt with his client's face on it, sat behind another white Ikea desk looking both curious and irritated. Davis was Asya Roc's manager and a partner in ARoc Productions.

"I'm wondering why you're here," Davis greeted.

"Three young men claiming association with this company stopped by my old office and placed this tag on my door." D handed over his phone.

Davis glanced at it and then handed it back.

"Is there a problem?" D asked.

"I don't know anything about this," Davis said. "Anyone could have tagged your door. This doesn't mean they were part of our crew."

"Let's cut the bullshit. I didn't tell the police anything and I'm not gonna implicate Asya. So please call off the toy thugs."

"I have no idea what you're talking about," Davis replied with a bored tone. "All I know is that we hired you the night of that attempted robbery. I heard you got him out of there, which I'm grateful for. But anything else I know zero about. I'm Skyping with Asya in France tomorrow morning, so I will ask him about it then."

"Okay," D said. "You tell him to chill out his posse. I'm sure the police are gonna talk to him about the shooting when he gets back. Just tell him that as long as he didn't see anything, I didn't either. I didn't have a bag and he didn't have a bag. If he's gonna tell the police anything, I need to know what. It would be best for all involved if we saw the same things."

"All right, I'll keep that in mind, and you should keep in mind that Asya has a lot of friends. He helps a lot of people on the street."

"And a lot on the Internet too, I see."

"That too. My point being—"

"Asya doesn't control them all."

"We're on the same page."

As D was leaving, Lynda Creed said, "You on Facebook, D?"

"Well, my company is. D Security. You wanna be my friend?"

"I'ma check your profile and see what's up."

D smiled at the young girl. Not only was that pleasant, D thought, but it could also be possibly useful. LC was too young for him, though she didn't seem to think so.

D was still smiling as he exited the building. Four loose-limbed, flat baseball–capped young black men sporting Asya Roc pendants crossed his path.

"Excuse me," D said.

"Yeah, you better," responded the smallest of the four.

As D took a few steps further, the tallest one said, "Yo, LeeLee, that's that nigga."

Three of the four quickly surrounded D with lots of "Yo, nigga!" chatter. Though all were smaller and collectively barely matched D's weight, the trio moved around him with confidence.

"Yo, ARoc is looking for you!" the one called LeeLee said, standing right in front of him.

"I was just up at the ARoc office. I left him a message."

"Them niggas up there don't know shit. *We* his people. We are who you need to speak to."

"Okay. You're LeeLee, right?"

"Yeah, that's me, nigga."

"Well, you tell Asya he'd better not snitch me out."

"*What*, nigga?"

"Tell him that I haven't said shit and he better not either. You got that?"

LeeLee was a little thrown off, as were his crew. They huddled quickly when the fourth kid, the one who'd stood a few steps away from the confrontation, called them over and started talking. LeeLee clearly wasn't happy but fell silent. The huddle broke and, as if D had disappeared, they walked right past him and into the building. LeeLee didn't even toss him a threatening glance.

* * *

That evening D was back in the Brownsville McDonald's with Ride, the former enforcer hanging on his words about Eryka and, of course, Eve.

"You think she lied to you?" Ride asked.

"I'm not 100 percent sure," D admitted, "but she was friendly enough that I don't think so."

"Yeah?" Ride smiled. "If she's as good as her little sis, you need to go tap that."

"Do you know this Detective Rivera?"

"Yeah, he arrested me."

"Well, I have somehow got connected to him."

Ride looked at him warily. "You working for him now?"

"Hell no," D said harshly. "But I do have some of his property. You think I can make a deal with him?"

"A deal? That spic nigga loves to squeeze people. He lives for that shit. My old homey got down with him; he bled him dry, then set him up. My man B. Brown is upstate and gonna be there another seven years. Me, personally, I would stay away from that dirty motherfucker. He's not just a cop. You feel me? Truth be told, he scares me. I can't go back in. I'd rather die. That nigga spic, he'd violate me and laugh while doing it. So that's what I know. D, you should stop whatever foolishness you got with Rivera. It ain't smart."

It was dark when D got off the 3 train from Brownsville at the Brooklyn Museum stop. He walked over to Islands, a tiny Jamaican spot not far from Eastern Parkway operated by two feisty middle-aged women who made the most succulent curried goat he'd ever had. So he waited patiently, cramped together with five other folks in a narrow waiting area, and then, sweaty from the oven's heat, paid for his takeout and headed home.

As he strolled down Washington, a Black Pearl taxi pulled parallel to him. D felt eyes on him. To his relief he spotted Ice in the back in a loose-fitting black-and-white Nets sweat suit. When D approached the vehicle, he saw crutches on the backseat floor.

"So," D greeted casually, "what it look like?"

Ice leaned up toward D and said, "I've been shanked worse than this. Get in."

When the car pulled away D said, "So, the guns, right?"

"Sure."

"My instinct was to dump them down the sewer."

"Understandable," Ice said.

"But I dropped them off somewhere."

"You did? Can you can get them?"

"Sure," D said. "Right now, if you want."

"No," Ice replied quietly. "Hold onto them. We both have questions, right?"

"A gang of them," D said. "Who goes first?"

"You can, but lemme help you. Far as I know, it was a straight-up sale. I brought the guns, the rapper had the cash. Shoulda been simple. I didn't set up the deal. One of my kids did. He'd hung with that rapper but felt it would be treated more professional if I handled things."

"So you were set up?"

"Not by him," Ice said. "Remember that thing that happened to your friend?"

D flinched at the reference to the death of Dwayne Robinson and the mess surrounding his book *The Plot Against Hip Hop*, especially coming from Ice, who knew most of the story and had much to do with its nasty ending. "I'll never forget it," D said.

"He was one of the kids involved and I kept him out of the light, so he owes me. But I think it was these other niggas up in Brownsville who he used to play dice with. Think he spoke too much. I'll deal with him. Believe: if I was robbing that rapper I would have called it off as soon as I saw you. Word is bond. Besides, if I was gonna do it I would have done it. I wouldn't have let those midget bangers handle my business."

"The police are very interested in you," D said. "Very."

"Until my leg is healed and I'm not limping, I'm out of state. That's the word on the street. Ice is out of state. If anyone asks, that's where Ice is."

"Shit, if anyone asks, I won't even know that."

"Understandable," Ice agreed.

"But what isn't understandable is why those two guys in the car were so committed to capping my ass. The guns must have been more valuable than they looked, cause those guys ended up dead behind them."

"Or they were just stupid," Ice said. "There's a lot of that goin' round. Niggas ain't thinking clearly. You pull a hammer, it would be wise to know how to fucking shoot it."

"Real talk," D said. "I still think you were being set up."

Ice looked out the window as the car cruised down Eastern Parkway. "So you moved back to Brooklyn?"

"It was time, I guess." D laid back, waiting to hear what his dangerous friend was thinking.

"Well," Ice said after a long pause, "I'm doing my own investigating. We'll compare notes real soon."

"What about the guns?"

"Leave them wherever you have them. The last thing I want is those things in my possession. I get caught with them and I'm upstate forever."

"So why'd you take the risk of making the delivery?"

Ice, usually poker-faced, gazed at D with a pained expression. "I got softhearted," he said bitterly. "Look what the fuck it got me. I'ma drop you off on Flatbush. The police or whoever may be on you, but I wanted to have this chat face-to-face. By the way, good looking out in that restroom. Despite this bullet I think I owe you, D. Could have been way worse."

"I'd say we're even."

"No." Ice was serious as a heart attack. "We aren't yet. You got the same e-mail?"

"Yeah."

"I'ma hit ya. If you get an e-mail from earthwindandfirethatass@gmail, it's me."

"Okay," D said, and got out of the Black Pearl happy to be, finally, headed home.

Live Like a King

The walls of the apartment were still white, but D had purchased several cans of a light-beige paint, thinking it would be soothing. Considering the police, the minigangstas, the OGs, and the general sense of disorientation in his life, *soothing* was a priority. He was watching Stephen A. Smith and Skip Bayless yell at each other on ESPN about some basketball recruiting controversy as he used Skype to call one of his family's oldest friends and his sometime savior, retired NYPD detective Tyrone "Fly Ty" Williams.

The old man's face appeared on his screen with new gray on his temples and deeper cervices in his reddish skin. Yet despite the morning hour, Fly Ty was looking good in a nylon knit sweater and Kangol cap.

"How's retirement?"

"Relaxing. Very relaxing. Twenty-four hours a day of relax."

"Bored out of your mind, huh?"

"Bored blind. Can't even see myself."

"Well I see you, Fly Ty. You look good. Can only see ten or eleven wrinkles. They say black don't crack but I can see that's not quite true."

"Ha. Well, D, I see every furrow in your supposedly young brow. You looking old, motherfucker."

"No doubt," D admitted. "Shit is hectic between the office closing, the move out of Manhattan, and all the stuff I e-mailed you about."

"It makes me wish I was back up in the Rotten Apple. Sounds like there's a lot of fun to be had getting you out of trouble."

"Can you do anything for me from down there?"

"There are still a few old heads at that precinct in Brownsville. I should still have a friend or two out there. Tell you what: you going out today?"

"I think my ass needs to stay home, don't you?"

"Okay. Let me get off this Internet and do some old-fashioned phone calling. Get back to you soon."

D started painting his living room and had applied a solid coat by the late afternoon. The Yankees, meanwhile, were behind by two runs during a day game in Detroit. He was having a bowl of microwaved lentil soup when another old blast from the past popped up on his BlackBerry.

"It's the great Al Brown!" D said gleefully into the cell. "The world's leading ancient-school road manager. To what do I owe this honor?"

Much like Edgecombe Lenox, Al Brown had begun in the business back when classic R&B singers walked the earth and soul didn't need "neo" tacked in front of it to make it relevant. "Night hasn't been on the road in seven years," he said.

"And hasn't put out a record in nine. So that's nearly a decade he's been out of the market," D replied.

Night was the great sphinx of R&B, a legendary talent who had become as infamous for his mysterious absences as Sly Stone or D'Angelo, gifted men who had the unfortunate habit of missing recording sessions and gigs, punctuated by arrests and teasing glimpses of greatness. D knew Night's backstory as well as anyone. He had been one of Night's best friends back when he dropped his landmark debut, *Black Sex*, a neosoul-meets-G-Funk mash-up that harmonized warring elements of popular black music. What Stevie Wonder had been to the '70s and Prince was to the '80s, critics and industry insiders predicted Night would be for the new millennium.

And it wasn't just music heads who dug Night. The video for his song "Untouched" featured a slow pan down his back, butt, and muscular legs that made Night a sensual sensation. Rumor had it that he had been a male prostitute for rich older women. Night denied it in interviews but D knew this was no rumor. It was the dark-chocolate truth.

"But the love is still there," Al said. "I know the fans are there and the music out in the marketplace hasn't gotten any better. There's still a space out there for him. I think even he knows that. But getting him to show up and on the tour buses and planes and into venues—he'll need help doing that."

"Sounds like you need a good assistant road manager more than a bodyguard."

"What Night needs, at least for this tour, is a supportive environment. We're hoping you can help with that. I'm sure you have some other commitments, but we have a short UK tour coming up. Just a week, really. You could do much worse."

"No question about that. I have absolutely done worse."

"I know you and Night have history."

"We do."

"I think he feels he owes you."

"I could see how he feels that," D said.

"Okay. Come to MSR Studios tonight. Don't show up too early, you know dude's a vampire."

When D got off the N train that night at 49th Street, he bumped and grinded through clumps of tourists down to "music row" on 48th Street where a bunch of music stars camouflaged the presence of several state-of-the-art recording studios, including MSR, a few steps from Seventh Avenue. Up in a third-floor studio, he sat on a sofa munching on almonds.

Night's Filipino engineer Reg was there, as was the assistant engineer, a young white kid named Carson, and Al, the singer's comanager, road manager, friend, and personal savior. It was a congenial group who'd worked together for years, bonded by a love of Night's music—though waiting on him had definitely worn them down.

"He said ten thirty," Al said blandly, "but that wasn't gonna happen."

D looked at his cell phone. Eleven fifteen p.m. "When do you guys usually start cutting?"

"One or one thirty. We're usually cooking by three a.m.," Reg said, then paused. "When he shows up."

"*If* he shows up," Al corrected.

Carson, the assistant engineer, came over and offered D a menu book. "If you don't mind eating late, there's lots of options around here after midnight."

"So," D said to Al, "we're settled in for the long haul."

"Funny. That's one of the potential titles for the album. *The Long Haul.*" They all chuckled. Then Al added, "Remember that old song 'Long-Ass Journey'?"

"Kinda."

"That's a possible title too. It's that old Adrian Dukes jam. He was a one-and-a-half-hit wonder and that was his half hit."

"Night is that self-aware?"

"He reads blogs just like everyone else," Al said.

To Carson, D said, "I'll just have a fruit salad."

"Watching your girlish figure?" Al asked.

"When you get older you are bound to put weight on. I just wanna control where it goes," D said. "By the way, Al, who's bankrolling all this? From what I hear, Night is six figures in debt to his label and they are through upping cash."

"We found someone who believes in Night as much as we do—except he has money."

"Who? Jay-Z?"

"Our sponsor wants to keep it on the low for now," Al said, sounding a bit cagey. "My feeling is that if Night makes it back, this guy will bask in the limelight. If it doesn't work out, no one has to know."

"Oooh," D said, "mysterious."

"Ours is not to ask why."

"Okay, it's dropped."

"Here he is," Reg chimed in.

On a monitor in the studio, Night could be seen being buzzed in from the street and walking languidly down a hall, guitar case in his left hand, can of Red Bull in his right. He had on baggy black jeans, working man's Timberlands, a garish Ed Hardy T-shirt that would have been cool in 2009, and his bushy hair was sticking out over the sides of his sky-blue bandanna. Night looked like a man just slightly out of sync with this era.

"It's only twelve forty-five," Al said. "You are in luck, D."

Night's team moved around the room, getting ready for their tardy star's arrival. It had been many years since D had spoken with the singer. He remembered when Night had been kidnapped by a slick-ass crew who rolled through New York City on Japanese rice rockets, running cars off the road, swarming people on the streets and city parks, and even raising havoc out on highway 27 through the posh Hamptons. That had been when Night was the hottest young voice in music, a sex symbol's sex symbol, leading R&B into the new millennium.

Night didn't stop in the control room to say hello, he just strode through a side door and into the studio, his brown eyes on the floor.

Al whispered, "That's a good sign. He wants to get to work. Otherwise he'd come in and shoot the shit until three a.m."

D hadn't noticed the vocal "cave" they'd created in the studio until Night ducked his head and disappeared into it. Using black tarp as a cover and mic stands held in place by gaffer's tape, Team Night had jerry-rigged a space separate from the drum set, keyboards, and monitors in the studio's main tracking area.

"When he's experimenting with his vocals he likes that privacy," Al told him. "He's got a humidifier in there, a keyboard, and some legal pads. When things are going well he works in there for hours."

For the next ninety minutes D sat with the others as the singer's dulcet tones emanated from his cave and flowed out of the studio speakers like pieces in a puzzle. The song in question was titled "Wallet, Cell Phone, Keys," which was also the hook and was followed by the line "What else a young man need?" (or "young woman," "young nigga," or "young bitch," depending on his mood). It was a sexy song about materialism that, if you didn't listen closely, could be heard as a celebration of it, an ambiguity that added great depth. It had the sophistication of a Stevie Wonder melody, the metaphorical splendor of a Rakim verse, and a sullen intensity solely of Night's making.

At some point during the session Al mentioned to Night that D was in the studio but the singer hadn't reacted. But after laying down some magical bits of melody over the lead vocal tracks, Night asked, "Is D still in there?"

"Right here on the sofa," Al replied.

"Send him in here."

D walked out of the control room and over a mess of scattered black wires into the cave. Standing up, with open arms, was Night. He gave D a big hug. D could smell the ripe scent of marijuana, funky armpits, and Red Bull all coming from the singer's body.

"It's been too long, Night."

"I know. I know, man." He laughed. "You looking good. Been liftin'?"

"Not like I want to," D said. "People think a guy who does what I do should be big up top, but it's not good being too muscle-bound."

"Shit, people think I should be working out like that too. Thing is, I thought I was supposed to be a musician. But I guess I was wrong."

"You gotta be you." D was trying to sound supportive.

"If I was really being me, there wouldn't be a biscuit or a waffle left in the state of Virginia. You feel me?"

D smiled and copped a squat on Night's monitor.

"So, you know, they want me to go over to London and do some shows," Night said.

"They love soul music over there and I know they love you."

"I haven't done a full-on show in seven years," Night said quietly.

"And?"

"And that shit worries the fuck out of me. People have their memories. I'm not that man anymore."

"Well," D said, "let them see who you are now. That's all any true artist can do. If they wanna see a ghost they can watch YouTube."

"It's a relentless beat, you know?" Night said. "The need for new shit, new sounds, new everything. That was the title of your man Dwayne Robinson's book: *The Relentless Beat.*"

"I know it well. Dwayne treated me like a son."

"Yeah, it was a shame how he got done. They ever catch those niggas?"

D looked the singer in the eye. "The streets did."

"Oh," Night said, surprised and a little unnerved, "like that, huh?"

"Yeah. I think there are some outstanding debts yet to be paid, but everyone who was involved is no longer above ground."

"Justice," Night said. He reached out and hugged D, who was getting a little teary. Night let him go and watched him closely.

"But," D said finally, "he's still dead."

"He was a smart man, D. Last few years, I read that book two or three times. I believe his whole theory about soul singers."

"The Fever."

"Yeah, 'The Fever.' That was a hell of a chapter."

In his book *The Relentless Beat*, the late Dwayne Robinson had written:

This Fever is not some benign three-day cold you can knock out with orange juice and aspirin. Once overcome by the Fever, it penetrates your DNA and alters your cell structure. Your sex appeal goes off the charts. Young girls scream. Adult women swoon. Even grandmothers get embarrassed by their sticky wet dreams. Sure, the transformation is amazing, but that doesn't mean it's all good. Once acquired, the Fever takes on a life of its own. Sex happens everywhere, all the time, until it loses meaning. You become insatiable and then the Fever consumes you. It wears out your body because too much fucking is like too much herb, too much candy, and too much food—it has nasty consequences. The Fever is what got Sam Cooke shot in a tacky LA motel. The Fever got Teddy Pendergrass crippled in a car accident. Because of the Fever, Eric Benét couldn't keep Halle. The Fever got Michael Jackson catching a case over some underage boy. The Fever got R. Kelly on film with an underage girl.

"I lived that whole theory out," Night said. "The singing, the women, and all that energy. It burned me up. It took me years to get myself back together. In Asia they have that concept of chi—the energy that animates your life and everything in the world. Your personal chi can get drained. Well, if chi was a cup of water, I was down to my last drop. You remember how I used to be? I could stay hard fucking a sixty-year-old white-haired bitch. That's how much chi I had."

"I remember you back in the day," D chuckled. "Crazy shit, Night."

"Yo," Night smiled and grimaced, like he wanted to laugh but had sore ribs, "you remember when I was brought in on suspicion of murder? They were gonna pin that shit on me. Then that crazy motorcycle posse kidnapped my ass. And that was all before I really was anything. But it was all outside me, you know? Once I had some hits, the shit was all about what was *inside* me. It was painful, D. It was real painful."

"Hey, that's all ancient history. The only thing that matters now is what happens next. The story continues cause life goes on."

"I'm trying, D."

"Motherfuckers used to call you the lost treasure of R&B. That was bullshit then and it's bullshit now. You are just a singer making a new record. All you need to do is sing well and write well. That's what you owe yourself. Not to me or Al or some woman screaming for you to take off your shirt."

Night laughed and patted his friend's shoulder. "You preaching tonight, D."

"No. This isn't about religion. You know I'm not the religious type. This is just what I know. I've spent a lot of time dwelling on shit that rained down on me. Can't keep wiping it off. Eventually, you gotta get new clothes."

"So," Night said, smiling, "when are you finally gonna stop dressing like an undertaker?"

"One thing at a time, motherfucker."

D saw Al and the production team waving at him from the control and nodded in their direction. "Maybe you should go make some more music before those guys out there fall asleep."

When D took his seat back on the control room sofa, Night said through the speakers, "D, this song is for you, my dude. It's how we should be." The track had a military rhythm reminiscent of Sade's "Soldier of Love," but with regal chords that suggested soul music meets the British royal court.

> *I'll battle anybody*
> *I'll do anything*
> *I fight like a lion*
> *And then live like a king*
> *I live like a king when I have no money*
> *I live like a king when the sun don't shine*
> *I live like a king cause the power is within me . . .*
> *[bridge]*
> *Living like a king isn't about my ego*
> *Living like a king isn't about objects*
> *Living like a king is a spiritual calling*
> *I live like a king cause I have no other options*
> *I live like a king to inspire my children*
> *I live like a king to make my own future*
> *I live like a king hoping you will join me*
> *And we'll all live like kings . . .*

When he finished the take, D told Al, "I am definitely feeling that."

Al smiled and patted D on his arm. "I am so glad you're here, D. We leave for London in two days. Dig out your passport."

FIRE WE MAKE

D hadn't gotten back to Brooklyn until five a.m. and, still wired by Night's music, didn't fall asleep until around six. So when Fly Ty hit him at ten a.m. he hadn't wanted to talk but his curiosity overpowered his fatigue.

Fly Ty popped onscreen looking serious with his light-blue Kangol on backward and his matching T-shirt. "I have some good news and some bad news. Actually, I have some small bits of good news and some large chunks of bad news."

"Okay. Let's start with the shoot-out."

"That's the very bad news. Not very, very bad, but it's up there. So the cops involved in the shoot-out did not put you in their paperwork. I had a friend look over their reports. When a member of the NYPD discharges their gun they get interviewed carefully. Internal Affairs really gets involved. Well, both were consistent. Maybe too consistent. Let me suggest why that is."

"Can't wait."

"Well, they weren't coming from the end of their regular shift. They, in fact, are part-time employees of a real estate company that seems to be buying up large parcels of land in Brownsville and East New York."

"Gentrifying the Ville? Damn."

"Real estate is a long game, D. Who knows what 2025 will look like."

"These guys are part-time brokers?"

"*Security and Community Relations Consultant* is how Rivera is listed. The other cop, Teddy Wynne, is hired by him on a freelance basis. But that does not explain why, if it went down as you said it did, they didn't include you in their reports."

"Nope," D said.

"But this bit of information may help explain things. The developers, AKBK Realty, sought these guys out. They are, apparently, the most corrupt crew in the precinct. They've been accused of protecting and extorting drug dealers. It's been said that they protect those baby pimps who kidnap girls and turn project apartments into brothels."

"So these are real bad boys?"

"Nothing's been proven but their rep is terrible," Fly Ty said.

"So maybe they didn't report me because they weren't sure what was in the bag and are worried, or because they were up to something themselves. Better to keep shit simple. You think they're looking for me?"

"I'd bet on it, and that's the very bad news."

D considered this a moment. "What should I tell those two detectives investigating the fight club thing?"

"Not sure. Let me check up on them first. But that guy Rivera—"

"He got the best look at me."

"Well, he may be bent but word is he's a good investigator and very smart. He's the one to worry about."

"They didn't actually do anything wrong. Truth is, they actually saved my ass."

"Nice of you to say that, but they may not feel that way. We don't really know what they'd just been into before you ran into them."

"I bet I interrupted something."

"Maybe. It's all speculation. But that's all I know now."

"What about the fight club thing?"

"Officially nothing happened. There was no report of any incident there. But people contacted the police with tips. They did find one shell casing. Off the record, they know someone got shot and that the casing matched a gun in a manslaughter case, but who knows how long that shell had been in the restroom? They also know Ice was somehow involved—anything about Ice gets them interested. Plus, they hear you and that rapper were involved too. Rapper perp walks are always popular. But they are not sure what really happened. There were three gunshot victims brought to Brookdale Hospital that night though none were shot in the leg. At King's County there were five admitted with gunshot wounds. Two leg wounds but they were both Hispanic teenage males. In essence they are looking for Ice and hoping he'll be looking for you and that'll you'll snitch."

"I saw Ice the other day," D said. "We're good. For a stone-cold killer he's a good dude, Fly Ty. But it's not comforting to know that the police are hoping he'll scare me into talking. It could give him bad ideas about me."

"Speaking of crazy motherfuckers, let's talk about your friend Mr. Ridenhour."

"Please. Whatcha got?"

"Well, he was upstate for felonious assault on a dealer with a baseball bat. He seems to have good judgment in these matters since he just broke the guy's arms and bruised his legs, but never hit him in the head and risked killing the guy. A very professional job."

"In case he comes at me with a Louisville Slugger, at least I know I'm in good hands. What about the girl?"

"Eve Wright. Thirty-one. Two shoplifting misdemeanors. One arrest for solicitation tossed. One divorce. Not from Mr. Ridenhour. New

York State driver's license. Address listed is 812 New Jersey Avenue."

"Great."

"Don't get your hopes up, I went on Google Maps. That building is undergoing some kind of renovation and is empty save a gang of hard hats."

"Ahhh."

"Also, she was born Eve Parsons but doesn't appear too loyal to that name. She also goes by Eva Peoples and Evelyn Patrick. Also been known to use her sister Eryka Wright's home. It's likely she's using a new name. I would if I had a big motherfucker just out of the joint in love with me."

"Maybe she owes him some cash? You think this is about money or love?"

"How should I know?" Fly Ty said. "He's your client."

"He's got a little guy following him around. About thirty. Lean, five nine, lemon-yellow with a goatee and small eyes. He's making the following obvious and Ride doesn't seem too concerned."

"Hmmm. You sure he's not actually a bodyguard?"

"I guess that's possible, though how this kid would keep that big motherfucker safe is a mystery."

"Let me see if there's some info I can find on known associates."

"Think you can help me find this old record?"

"I'm a lifelong cops-and-robbers guy," Fly Ty replied. "I like music as much as the next man. But searching out lost vinyl? That's not what I do. Too bad your man Dwayne Robinson isn't around. This probably would have been a no-brainer for him."

"Yup. No question about that . . . I have an idea."

"Ideas are good. Strong locks on your door would help too. Just in case you get some unexpected visitors."

"You mean *more* of them."

"Ahh," Edge said wistfully, "Brooklyn."

D woke back up around three p.m. He did push-ups, sits-ups, and some stretching. He washed down his HIV meds with apple juice and then had his usual breakfast of oatmeal and almond butter. He filled his black Tumi suitcase with clothes, shoes, and toiletries, happily contemplating getting out of town; the money he'd receive would pay three months' rent. Between Ride's cash, the Rihanna payment, and the unexpected Night windfall, this had been his best month in quite a while. He wanted to get D Security rolling again and this move to Brooklyn, though action-packed, was proving profitable.

Finished with his packing, D decided to have a bit of fun.

He used social media much like every borderline middle-aged man. He got into the occasional Twitter fight with other basketball fans over LeBron vs. Jordan, the Knicks' deficiencies, and whether the great sight lines at the Barclays Center made up for the supertight upper-deck seating. (D, in fact, chided Jay-Z about that very thing one night when he was bodyguarding him, and the MC's reply was, "Lose weight.")

D also surfed Facebook for photos of hot women who felt it was their social media duty to post shots of themselves in all manner of revealing clothes, from two-piece swimsuits to Victoria's Secret knockoffs to curve-hugging stretch pants. D wasn't proud of this preoccupation but sometimes his private life felt a bit Spartan and this online Peeping Tom bit harmlessly spiced things up.

Because of his music business connections, D received weekly friend requests from singers around the country (and sometimes the world) seeking management, a record deal, publicity, or some other hookup. If their profile picture appealed to him, D would check out their music link, and if—and only if—they could sing or had good songs he'd review their photo albums. It was, he felt, a way to maintain some integrity and not be just another horny Facebook stalker. (This was bullshit but it justified his habits.)

He had recently received a friend request from a woman named Cassie Wilson, a cute dark-brown sister with big eyes and sexy Chaka Khan vocals. She was from the Bay Area but lived in Los Angeles, and she performed in a medley of body-hugging, low-cut, Beyoncé-lite dresses that D found quite appealing.

In one photo Cassie was at the microphone with a honey-colored, natural red-haired singer named Eva who caught D's eye. Though more modestly dressed than her friend, D thought her sparkling eyes and taller frame more beautiful. So he clicked on Eva's page where there was a picture of a lovely California sunset and a profile shot of Eva with a reality star–level brunette weave.

In Eva's photo albums there were a bounty of images sure to warm the heart of any soft-core cyberpeeper: workout shots in formfitting gear, bikini shots in Mexico, and selfies in various bedroom and bathroom mirrors. There was an album titled "Throwbacks" that D clicked on because of an adorable cover shot of a non-glammed-up Eva, probably taken more than five years earlier. Unlike the Los Angeles lifestyle shots that filled Eva's other Facebook albums, these pictures were taken in New York and featured a chubbier, more baby-faced Eva in Baby Phat fashions.

Then, in a picture dated 2003, Eva sat on the hood of a car in the arms of hulking man in a blue Yankees jacket and matching baseball cap. D clicked on the photo but the man was listed simply as, *My old boo!* It appeared to be taken in New York and the huge brother definitely could have been Ride. A search of his wallet, desk, and the boxes accumulated since he'd moved back to Brooklyn didn't yield the photo that Ride had given him in the Brownsville McDonald's. He was supposed to meet Ride there again in three days, but now he'd be in London and he had no way to reach him.

D e-mailed Ray Ray a link to Eva's page and told him to meet with Ride for him and to show him the Facebook page. It would be sweet, he thought, to have actually found something he was asked to find. Ray Ray, as it turned out, must have been e-mailing him at the same time, because he received two large attachments from the kid. *Watching Rivera* was the subject line. Ray Ray wrote: *After what we saw at the beauty shop and your story I decided to follow Rivera around the Ville. I caught him ass-out a couple of times.*

The first file was a video taken two days before on Ray Ray's phone. Rivera came out of the AKBK Realty office at night with a sack over his back like he was some ghetto Santa Claus. He walked down Livonia Avenue and then up a side street, which had an empty lot and some crumbling homes. The detective used keys to open the back basement door of one of those unsightly structures. The camera was moving toward the house when it stopped suddenly and ducked down. Two teenagers on bikes appeared at the basement door and the video cut off. When it started again the camera peered through a basement window as the two teens fondled 9mm pistols. Rivera sat watching them while sucking on a vapor cigarette. Then the video ended.

In the second video, Rivera walked down Livonia Avenue with a small orange grocery bag in his right hand, the kind you usually brought vegetables home in. The camera followed him from across the street. At one point the cop made a furtive turn of his head that suggested he might know he was being watched as he entered AKBK Realty, right before the video cut off.

Two minutes later D was speaking harshly into his BlackBerry: "What the fuck are you doing?"

"I got that nigga, don't I, D?" Ray Ray was bubbling with excitement.

"Did he see you?"

"I don't think so."

"I think he did," D snapped, like a scolding father. "Does he know you?"

There was a long pause. "Kinda."

"Kinda how?"

"He knows my mother."

Does that mean he fucked her? D thought. "Shit. He ain't sentimental. He'd shoot you or set you up as fast as the next man."

Ray Ray wasn't scared; he sounded righteous. "He's selling guns out here, D. He's arresting people and getting them killed at the same time. He's making his own business. Somebody will wanna know that."

"Promise me you will not follow this man again. This is more than enough."

"Cool. But what should we do? Bloomberg ain't mayor no more and Kelly ain't top cop."

"And Brooklyn has a black DA. Yeah. Yeah. It all sounds good, but between the people at the top and us at the bottom there are a lot of layers." D was getting increasingly emphatic. "Do not show this to anyone else, okay? No one. Not your mother. *No one.* I'll be out of the country one week. We'll come up with a plan when I get back."

"Gotcha, yo," Ray Ray said. Then, in a small voice, "We gonna get him, right?"

"Let's hope he doesn't get us first."

FEENIN'

That evening D got in a good workout at the Eastern Athletic club on Eastern Parkway near Grand Army Plaza, his new gym. He did a lot of upper-body work and then thirty minutes on the stationary bike for cardio. He didn't usually do a ton of stretching, but knowing there was a long plane trip the next day he did some basic yoga poses and a shoulder stand. Walking out into the warm early spring evening, D felt really good.

From where he stood D spied the black bars around the Botanic Garden. The guns were in there. D knew he should have just ditched them that night on Utica Avenue. He hoped he wouldn't regret that decision.

As he walked up Eastern Parkway he clocked some furtive movements in the passenger-side mirror of a parked Hyundai. After he passed the vehicles, a man emerged and moved swiftly toward D in sneakered feet. D slid one arm out of the backpack he was carrying his gym gear in, as if he was about to unzip a pocket. Instead, he twisted his torso like a kickboxer and flung it toward his attacker's surprised face.

The first bullet whizzed by D as the flying backpack obscured the shooter's vision. A second bullet hit the sidewalk to his right, bouncing off the pavement and shattering the windshield of an innocent BMW.

D came at the shooter in a bum-rush, launching his body and knocking the guy back onto the unforgiving Brooklyn concrete. The shooter's lungs deflated like a balloon and the back of his head drizzled red like a broken ketchup bottle. The man, who looked to be in his early twenties with reddish-brown skin, wasn't dead, but dude was far from healthy. Next to him was a Beretta and two spent shell casings, one of which was rolling toward the curb.

Lights came on up and down Eastern Parkway and the car alarm in the BMW whined.

"Who sent you?" D shouted. "Who?"

D's interrogation went nowhere as the shooter oozed out of consciousness. So he patted the pockets of the guy's skinny jeans, finding a worn leather wallet with a 24 Hour Fitness membership, a New York State–issued ID card, and a Social Security card, each bearing different names (Akil Simpson, Ahmir Salmon, Alvin Sims). In another pocket was a roll of bills that, by D's quick count, amounted to several hundred dollars. D slipped the wallet and cash back in his attacker's pockets as the first patrol car pulled up.

Though he had been the target of an attack, D soon found himself seated in an interview room of the local precinct with a chai latte on the table before him and one-way glass in front of him. He'd given his statement to a patrolman and offered the investigating detectives what little information he knew (save his quick inspection of Akil/Ahmir/Alvin's pockets). A couple of phone calls later D had been asked to accompany the cops to the station and he'd agreed, figuring a police precinct sit-down had been in the cards ever since the fight club incident with the guns.

So when Detective Mayfield appeared, in a blue-and-orange Mets T-shirt and baggy jeans, with a badge dangling from a chain and a file in his hairy hands, D actually relaxed. "Remember me, Mr. Hunter? Detective Mayfield. Hope you aren't too shaken up to answer a few more questions."

"Not at all," D said.

A moment later a frowning Detective Robinson entered the room in a suit and tie, like a great night out on the town had been cut short.

"Looking good, Detective Robinson," D said.

The cop leaned back against the wall. "Please don't kiss our ass, Hunter." His voice was acid. "Looks like you brought some Brownsville shit to Prospect Heights. We're not having that."

"Well," D countered, "I'm the victim here, detectives. Some fool wanted to mug me right here in New Brooklyn."

"Mugging Hunter?" Robinson said. "Feels like a hit to me."

"I have that same feeling," Mayfield added. "Lots of guns go off around you, Hunter. You don't seem to be so good at keeping yourself secure."

"You guys know more than I do, apparently," D said.

Robinson, smelling of CK One cologne, came over to the table. "Your pal Ice probably set this up. He knows you could get him sent away. The gun-possession laws in this town are pretty strong. Just say what you saw. Don't make a thing up. Just speak the truth."

"Well, maybe you should speak to Ice and find out why he picked me."

"We will," Mayfield said, "but we think you're a little too smart to think Ice would let a guy like you have something like this to hang over him."

"Besides," Robinson cut in, an edge of anger in his voice, "shouldn't he be worried that you'd be spooked after this 'random' attack and then come in and make some kind of deal with us? Unless he has something on you, Hunter. Maybe *you* are the bad guy in all this."

D stood up. "Well, detective, I am not a lawyer but I got a strong feeling I have no reason to be here any longer. I gave my statement—can I go?"

"Don't make us wait too long, Hunter," Robinson said.

D momentarily wondered if he should have mentioned to the two detectives that he was about to leave the country, but then thought, *Hell no,* and ran back to his apartment in a hard sprint.

A Change Is Gonna Come

D worried that United Kingdom customs was gonna be a problem for Night. The singer's various run-ins with the law in
his lost years and being labeled a "hip hop artist" by the UK press had
led to him being denied entry in the past. Snoop Dogg's troubles came
to mind as D, Night, Al, and the band took the long, winding walk at
Heathrow Airport from their plane to customs after their overnight
flight.

Al assured him that Night's mystery manager had smoothed things
out via the US State Department. Nonetheless, D was fully prepared to
be detained with Night and put on the plane back to JFK. As they came
into the wide customs room there were lines for EU passport holders
and non–EU passport holders to small podiums manned by thirtyish
agents wearing white quasi-military shirts and blankly bureaucratic
expressions.

As the mostly white, well-heeled first- and business-class passengers led the way and the economy passengers filed behind them, Al
guided his charges into the non-EU line, whispering to Night as they
moved. Apparently the singer harbored the same fears as D, and Al, as
usual, was a calming force.

Sitting in chairs to the side, looking forlorn with a mountain of luggage, were two African families in flowing traditional garb with plenty
of kids in tow. There was also a Middle Eastern family with the mother
in a blue burka; the father was talking to the two African men. They

exchanged a few words and then quietly laid out their prayer mats and got on their knees. D wasn't sure how they knew which direction faced east, but the trio, already detained for reasons unknown, were not shy about displaying their devotion to Allah even when it could be one more reason to deny them entry.

D watched Night walk up to the podium and greet the customs officer, a chubby white woman wearing too much early-morning eyeliner. She gave Night a once-over and then scanned his passport through a computer. She peered at the screen as D and Al nervously looked on.

"Next, please." A different customs officer was gesturing for D to come forward. He had just asked D some rote questions ("What brings you to England? . . . How long will you be here?") when they both heard Night singing Sam Cooke's "A Change Is Gonna Come." His tenor floated across the large space, turning heads, altering the room's molecules.

The female customs officer was beaming as Night sang the civil rights anthem. A stern-faced supervisor stood close by, not amused, though most of his employees seemed pleased. "Change" isn't really a clap-along song but a couple of travelers, enthused and off-rhythm, started doing just that. The claps spread around the room.

A feel-good moment turned magical when one of the detained African men began to sing with Night. D thought the man Senegalese or maybe from Mali because of his keening high-pitched tone. Night heard the guy and began to harmonize. One of the African's daughters, a tiny thing in pink sneakers, tried to add her small voice but her mother hushed her quiet. The African didn't know all the words but seemed to know the melody. The two men adjusted to one another in that awkward concert hall. It was strange; it was timeless.

And then it was over. Night had run out of lyrics and was starting to riff off the melody when Al gave him the "cut" sign and Night shut it down. Charmed, the customs lady applauded and stamped his passport, her day made. The African father put his hands back in prayer and nodded to Night, who, genuinely moved, nodded back before Al escorted him down an escalator to baggage claim.

"What made you do that?" D asked when he'd caught up.

"Honey wasn't sure about me," the singer said. "I didn't know if she was gonna let me in. My face—shit, my whole body—was a lot skinnier when I took that passport photo. I told her I was in England to sing. She said, *Prove it.* So I did."

"See what happens when you do what you do best?" Al said.

"You think they gonna let that family in?" Night asked.

"Hard to tell," D said. "I'm not sure him singing with you was his best move."

"It worked for me," Night said.

"But you are clearly coming in to entertain and make someone British some money," D said. "That brother there, with all his luggage and kids, looked like he was there to settle down. Don't think the Brits are checking for any more Muslims."

"Damn," Night said, "black folks catching hell everywhere."

"Since when haven't they?" Al said, wise white man that he was.

After his impromptu performance at Heathrow, Night fell asleep in the taxi into London. Al dozed off too. But D, who'd napped fitfully on the flight, was awake, a bit electrified by his return to London. It was about six a.m. and rush hour was just creeping to life. The ride in from the airport to Central London rolled across Brompton Road, past the Victoria and Albert Museum into the shopping mecca of Knightsbridge, tipping its hat to the vast superstore that is Harrods and past massive Hyde Park, where marble statues of lost empire loomed over passing traffic.

Heading around the park's border toward Marble Arch, D spied men standing on small makeshift platforms railing against the British government, Jews, Muslims, Apple, Microsoft, the United States, and other evils. This was Speakers' Corner, a venerable London tradition where on Sunday mornings folks filled with grievance attacked the powers-that-be and the powers-imagined-to-be. Years ago, when he'd traveled to London with Jay-Z, D spent a fun blustery morning watching Palestinians, Israelis, Serbs, Hindus, and Irishmen, all with British accents, drown each other out.

The taxi cut down Oxford Street, a popular strip of department stores, fast food, sidewalk vendors, and money exchangers that reminded D of Manhattan's 34th Street. Across from the Bond Street tube station the taxi turned into a cul-de-sac, stopping in front of the Berkshire Hotel, a spot with small rooms, narrow beds, big bathtubs, and decent prices. It wasn't a rock star's hotel but a modest place perfect for a man rehabbing his career. Al handled the check-in and quietly slipped D a key to Night's room ("Just in case").

It was nine thirty a.m. when D's head hit the pillow and three fifteen p.m. when his eyes reopened to the sounds of a busy Central London. After a hot, relaxing soak in a deep bathtub, D called Al. Soundcheck was at five thirty p.m. Al hadn't called Night yet but figured they'd go round him up together.

When they knocked on Night's door around five, they heard stirring and hushed voices. Al and D traded looks.

A petite, curvy, light-brown beauty opened the door and said, "Hello," with the "H" missing.

"I remember you," Al said.

"Yes," she replied. "I'm Kira Paris Sanders and I still run this town."

"I'm sure you do."

They hugged and then D introduced himself.

She turned to him and said, "You were here with Jay-Z, weren't you?"

"Yeah," D said, surprised.

"I always remember a tall man."

"I don't know how I missed you."

"Jay had you busy," she said. "But it's still your fault we never met."

Night, to D's further surprise, came to the door fully dressed. "You know what they call this girl? Kira is the motherfucking Queen of Clubs."

"Okay," D said, taken aback by her beauty and confidence, and the respect Al and Night accorded her.

In the van to soundcheck D got some of the woman's backstory. Her family was from Eritrea, an East African country D had heard of but had no idea where it was. (Al explained that Eritrea is a little piece of land squeezed up next to Ethiopia and Somalia.)

Kira wasn't known as London's Queen of Clubs for promoting parties, but for having the city's hottest posse of girlfriends, a group so fly she'd started a booking agency—where her crew was paid for showing up at parties and sitting at tables loaded with complimentary bottles— and published a calendar featuring posse members in bikinis around London. Kira called the calendar "London's Queens," and it sported models with roots in Africa, the Caribbean, Asia, and even Eastern Europe. The calendar was cheekily subversive, as it suggested that twenty-first-century United Kingdom beauty was far removed from the pale fair maidens of yore.

Kira wasn't shy about popping her collar, which amused Night and Al—though D was on the fence about her. Whenever you hit a new city on tour, it was good to connect with old friends and folks who knew what was happening (and what wasn't). But Kira was a straight-up party girl and D was concerned that she might drag Night back into his bad habits.

Everybody loved playing Ronnie Scott's. The venerable Soho night-club opened in 1959 and had hosted jazzmen, soul stars, and rockers of every stripe in the ensuing decades. When Night was a young phenom-enon, he'd played two historic nights at Ronnie Scott's and recorded a live EP that included covers of the Ohio Players, Earth, Wind & Fire, and Eddie Kendricks that had the local press dubbing him "the future of soul music."

It hadn't quite worked out that way, but Al still thought it was wise to bring him back to the club, a place that would inspire good memories in a man who needed to recall how great he could be. Old hands at Ronnie Scott's came out to hug and greet Night, but also seemed just as excited to see Al. He was part of a brotherhood of road dogs, people for whom the sour smell of dried spilled beer, the soft, mushy feel of dirty carpets, and the floating dust of rooms not meant to be seen in sunlight made them bark and wag their tails.

As the band set up for soundcheck, Night yawned heavily and be-gan playing chords on the electric piano. D was settling in at a table by the bar to wait on the venue's security head when Kira came over, pulled out her phone, and snapped a photo of him.

"I'm Instagramming you."

"Really."

"Yes, big guy. My friends want to see you."

"Should I be scared?"

"Very." A moment passed. Kira looked at her phone and said, "My friend Gem wants to know if you know how to party properly."

"Listen," he said sternly, "you seem sharp and like a fun person. I'm sure your girls are too. But partying properly is not what I'm in London to do and certainly not why Night is here. Partying properly is why he hasn't performed here in ten years. You feel me?"

"Completely," Kira replied. "I totally understand. I said to Night this morning he needs to be good. I've kept in contact with him over the years and have great affection for him. I brought him breakfast this morning and we talked about his life. For your info, we aren't lovers. I'm just a good friend."

"That's between you and him," D said.

"Well, now it's between me and you, big man."

The security chief came over and D left with him to tour the backstage area, but Kira stayed on his mind. She had crossed D's personal line. Since he'd been infected with the HIV virus some fifteen years earlier, D had pretty much kept his dick to himself. His last real lover had been murdered a couple of years ago in a ghastly crime where a suicide had been faked and she'd been injected with the HIV virus in a sick message to D.

Kira's approach disturbed him, particularly since he felt it was just a tease, the woman striking him as someone who wanted to seduce every man in her vicinity just to feed her ego. D was determined not to join that club. *Good luck with that*, he thought to himself.

The soundcheck went a bit long as Night and the band slowly pushed through jet lag. Night guided the band through some tunes as many as five times and was as hard on himself as he was on his players. Kira disappeared at some point, which lightened D's mood.

Instead of heading right back to the hotel, Al took Night, D, and the band over a couple of blocks from Ronnie Scott's to Busaba Eathai, a hip Thai place with healthy food, long wooden tables, and ambient lighting. As D downed chicken satay, brown rice, and a Thai salad, Al took a phone call and then leaned over.

"The manager's gonna be here tonight," he said to D. "He's flying in for the show."

"No name for me yet?"

"No," Al said, "but I think you'll be impressed."

"His money seems good and he got me a trip to London. Unless he's Satan or Elvis returned, I'm good."

"Hey," Al said, nodding his head, "check it out."

A pair of redheads who looked like sisters in their early thirties, who were dressed like they were on their way to the theater, recognized Night and were apologizing that they weren't seeing his gig at Ronnie Scott's later that night.

The slightly taller redhead said, "We played 'Black Sex' until the CD skipped. It was so frustrating."

Night's smile, the thousand-watt light that had once made him a successful hustler, was shining at his two UK fans, though his teeth were closer in color to American cheese than pearly white. D used the other woman's cell to take a picture that captured their moment with the revived spirit of R&B.

Back at the hotel, after a hundred push-ups, sixty sit-ups, some stretching, and another hot bath, D slipped on his black suit, ready for the night. His UK cell buzzed.

It was Al: "Come down to the lobby in ten."

Sitting in the small lobby of the Berkshire Hotel was Amos Pilgrim, legendary black music power broker, successful former label head, and Night's manager. The last time D had seen Pilgrim he'd punched the man dead in his face.

"So," D said, standing over the man, "I assume you are firing me."

"What makes you say that? Our history?"

"Of course."

"Please sit down." Reluctantly D sat across from Pilgrim. "Our history has nothing to do with Night. I've already invested well over $100,000 in studio time, rehearsal time, and tour support. I want to make that money back and you're gonna help me. In fact, you've already helped me."

"And why would I help you?"

"Cause I got a feeling I could help *you* with a few matters."

"The last time I saw you it didn't end well. We supposed to be friends now?"

"Well, my plastic surgeon was very happy for the work," Pilgrim said, trying to break the ice. "Let that stay in the past. Some parts of the past are useful, some aren't. D, I hear you are doing a great job with Night. I want that to continue."

"Glad you feel that way," D said. "I won't be working for you after this trip."

"Whatever suits you." Pilgrim stood up and offered his right hand.

D stood too, slowly shook Pilgrim's hand, and then walked out of the hotel into the early-evening hustle of Oxford Street.

A few minutes later he arrived at Shaftesbury Avenue after exiting the Starbucks next to the tube station, taking in the tumult of double-decker buses, folks with accents from Jamaica, Africa, and the West End, plus the universal hard-edged sound of hustlers talking shop, augmented by music from passing cars, shops, and leaking out of headphones. D sipped his chai latte and tried to suppress his disgust at this nasty turn of events. He knew Night could use his presence and he surely needed Amos Pilgrim's cash and contacts. But D had quickly decided it would be enough to get his old friend through this brief tour.

* * *

Later that night, standing stage left at Ronnie Scott's, D tried to let the music drown out his ill will toward Pilgrim. He could see the portly mogul at a table with two white Englishmen talking a mile a minute. The place was packed. R&B–loving London was in the house, but D's mind was back in the USA, deep in unpleasant memories of friends and lovers dead—tragic events that Pilgrim, inadvertently, had helped trigger.

By the time D refocused on the show, Night had finished his second encore, the small club was roaring, and the singer was soaking up the love. D manned the door to the crowded dressing room as UK soul heads, some of the most dedicated music fans on the planet, clamored for access.

Kira soon appeared with two friends—a short, thick Nigerian woman with exceedingly dangerous curves named Gem, whose dark-chocolate skin glowed, and Solonge, a Somalian Amazon with brown eyes as round as Big Ben and a short dress that showcased long cinnamon legs.

"We are taking you all out tonight," Kira announced. "It's all been arranged."

"No doubt," D said happily.

First stop was a club down the block from the Ritz hotel, which felt like a slick Big Apple spot except that the athletes in tight shirts played for Chelsea and Arsenal, not the Knicks and Giants, and the girls in stupendous heels and big hair were from Croydon, not Jersey.

As Al and D watched like hawks, Night filled his cup with cranberry juice minus the vodka. Pilgrim sat with him, drinking Cokes in solidarity with his client, while Kira's ever-growing crew of Brit beauties made up for what the drinks lacked. D, who stood at the end of the banquette, felt two soft hands embrace his head. A voice whispered, "See, we are being good with Night."

"Good girl," he replied.

"But you other guys do not party properly," Kira said, after letting go of his head and moving in front of him.

"Sorry to disappoint."

"It's still early. You have the rest of the night to make it up to me."

After ninety minutes at the club, Kira rounded up the Americans and a core crew of cuties for a trip to Mayfair, a posh section of London. Once there, they descended into a subterranean space where rich Europeans were carousing to EDM mixes of Adele and Ibiza hits by Skrillex and Avicii. The group squeezed through the main room into an alcove in a small, raucous private space.

D stood to the left of the alcove, looking professional as a bacchanal of boogying butts bounced to bodacious beats. Kira and Gem danced in front of D, oozing like lava a foot before him and then rubbing back on him, enjoying the volcano they wished to erupt. Night laughed and pointed at D, as entertained by his bodyguard's crumbling poker face as by the ladies' gyrations.

Hours passed, and at about three a.m., everyone was spread around the Berkshire lobby. They'd picked up three cheeky white girls at the Mayfair club and an ebony-and-ivory party was underway. Night gave D a look and soon the bodyguard was escorting Gem and one of the white girls up in the tiny hotel elevator, the singer intoxicated by lust and a few hits of herb as he cupped the asses of both his companions.

Whatever the trio got into was none of D's business, especially after he'd closed the door behind them and slid the *Do Not Disturb* sign on the doorknob. Feeling liberated, jet-lagged, and in need of privacy, D went back to his own room, plopped on the bed, and channel surfed until he found an NBA game between the Knicks and the Nets. He couldn't tell if it was live or prerecorded, but it was soothing to hear the American accents. He closed his eyes and let the basketball commentary fill his ears.

There was a soft, insistent knock. D tried to ignore it but the sound didn't stop, so the big man stumbled from his bed to the door.

She stood there, fluttered her eyes in a parody of coquetry, and said, "Good morning," before pushing past him as if he was air. "It seems my friends have abandoned me." Kira sat on his bed. "Tried to find an off-license taxi but had no luck." She opened the minibar door, sliding out a small champagne bottle that she popped opened with a bartender's aplomb. "Hope you don't mind, but I figure you won't drink it."

D finally closed the door and found a spot on the other end of the bed as he tried the impossible—not to be drawn to her powerful spirit.

"I just want to sleep. Is that all right with you, luv?"

"I dunno," D said, and locked his eyes back on the Knicks and Nets. Soon he was horizontal on the bed and Kira was curled up, cat cute, on his chest, her eyes open but looking far away.

Morning light slid through cracks between the window and shades, dancing across Kira's face as she slept. D slowly awakened to find he was topless and she had bits of her clothing off too. He had the acute sense he'd somehow missed the party. His right hand was cupping one of her ass cheeks; it was the sweetest, most tender thing. Then D found himself kissing it, feeling that skin on his lips and then tongue. Kira murmured, coming slowly alive, eyes closed but her mouth smiling and then open, gasping for air. His nose nestled between her ass cheeks as his lips lingered on the wet places between her legs.

Several minutes later there were heavy feet outside the door and then a sliding sound. D tilted his head and saw an envelope had been slipped into the room. Kira turned and twisted, grabbed his head, and breathed so very deeply. D wiped his face and rose from the bed.

It was an invitation-sized envelope with fine paper and a stamped seal—some new age–looking image that commingled an English lion with a computer keyboard. Inside was a handwritten note:

Welcome to London. You have been in my employ via the esteemed Mr. Lenox for some time now. I'd love to meet with you for tea and conversation. My driver will be by at one p.m.
Yours truly,
Sir Michael Archer

"A royal invitation from the Queen?"

"No, I think it's from a count or duke."

"Nice. In London two days and already in with the royals."

"I thought *you* were the Queen."

"I am," Kira affirmed. "I order that you bow down again."

"Kneel at your throne?"

"Yes, head down, please."

"As you wish, Your Highness."

OTHERSIDE OF THE GAME

There was nothing overtly sinister about Sir Michael Archer. He was a round-faced, red-nosed man with skin as ruddy as a well-trod country road; his eyes were steel blue and lined with red veins like cracked eggshells. It was the face of a pub bartender, D thought, not a master of any universe. And yet, he'd made millions.

"There was a magical time in your country, a time when you had giants walking among you," Archer said. "All this talent that came of age after World War II. You had Miles Davis and Chuck Berry. You had Mahalia Jackson and John Coltrane. Do you know who these people are?"

"Yes."

"Have you ever listened to them?"

"I have never heard much gospel," D admitted. "I know Coltrane's *Giant Steps*. I know Chuck Berry when I hear his music."

"Ignorant, aren't you?"

"Excuse me?"

"Ignorant of your legacy is what I mean," Archer explained. "A sad disease often prevalent amongst Americans, but now so widespread it's like your people had nothing to do with all that great art."

"You need to stop that *your people* shit."

"But are you not one of the blacks of North America? Heirs to a great culture that you know little or nothing about?"

"I'm no historian but it is *our* culture." D was getting hot. "Our grandparents and parents made it and we can treat it any way we want."

"When something isn't treasured, it is up for grabs, my friend. I mean, who really owns a thing after it's out in the world—the creator, the heirs, or its owners?"

"You don't own black people or black culture any more than me wearing a bespoke suit means I own Britishness or whatever the fuck you call it over here."

"No need for anger, my friend. Let me show you something." Archer rose and started walking, taking for granted that D would follow.

The estate was forty minutes outside Central London, with a big ornate gate, a long driveway, a fountain out front, and endless rooms filled with drapery, portraits of dead ancestors, and an old suit of armor. It was a *Masterpiece Theatre* house that made D as uncomfortable as Archer's arrogant demeanor.

Down a narrow staircase and through a heavy door into a basement that was brightly lit. The hum of an air conditioner was loud. D hadn't seen so much vinyl in years. Shelves of records from floor to the fifteen-foot ceiling. The stacks went far back, like the warehouse in *Citizen Kane*. In *Kane*, the valuables had been gathered from around the globe, a testament to his travels and money. These possessions had not been looted from third world countries, but were booty from not so long ago, when a man could traverse the world going from record shop to record shop. LPs, many of them still wrapped in plastic, were stacked in neat rows with little tabs every four or five feet identifying labels: Motown, Capitol, Stax, Blue Note, Atlantic, Philly International, and smaller tabs for individual artists.

If you were seeking Coltrane, for example, you'd have to look under the Impulse, Blue Note, and Atlantic labels—the pedigree of the record company had as much weight in how these recordings were organized as the artist on the cover. It reminded D of the old Colony Records in

Times Square but with greater detail. Even LA's humongous Amoeba Music was no match for the immensity and meticulousness of Archer's collection.

"Would you like to see my 45s?"

D just nodded, overwhelmed by the dedication—fanaticism, really—that this collection embodied.

Through a red door with three locks and down a short, dimly lit corridor was a room lined with facsimiles of bank-vault security boxes, but sized to accommodate 45rpm records. There were over a hundred of them built into three of the room's four walls.

"Look at this." Archer gestured toward the wall on D's right. Every security box on that side bore the Tamla/Motown logo, with serial numbers underneath. "It is every one of their singles from 1959 to 1972." He seemed awed by his own acquisitions. "A golden age never duplicated before or since."

Archer walked over to an eye-level box and, using a key, opened it, sliding out the first 45. He handed it over to D. It was the Miracles' "Shop Around."

"Impressive," D said.

"Yes. That was Motown's first hit record. My collection is vast, but it is incomplete."

Archer took the ancient Miracles record from D and slid it back in its place, then secured the box.

"You see," he said, turning to face D, "I'm not some evil man trying to control black history. I am just obsessed with keeping, no pun intended, a record. Very few people in the world care about this music and the culture that produced it more than I do."

"Or," D replied, "you just have the cash to collect and build something like this and too much time on your hands."

"People think money is about objects," Archer said. "So they fix-
ate on buying the shiny and new. But what money is really good for is
unleashing your passion. At least that's what it is for me. It has freed me
to be more of who I am."

"You could also say you are trapped by the past and this place is a
very nice prison."

Archer laughed. "For a bodyguard, you have a rather dour view of
success, D. Occupational hazard?"

D looked around the 45 room, taking it all in since he expected to
never see it again. Then he said, "Life experience."

"Would you like more tea, D?"

On the ride back to London, D took stock of his trip. It had been brief,
but so much had happened in a few days. Night's confidence was re-
turning. Suddenly the scheming Amos Pilgrim was back in his life. Plus,
he found himself working for another arrogant (damn near imperialist)
businessman. And, of course, there was the disturbingly sensual Kira,
who would surely dominate his dreams for years to come.

He'd actually stopped thinking about all that mess back in Brooklyn. He hadn't checked his phone messages or even looked at his e-
mail. Ice, Rivera, etc. were an ocean away. He'd decided it would all
stay over there until he returned home.

After three nights at Ronnie Scott's, Night and company headed
north to Birmingham, a hard, working-class city that was now filled
with West Indians, Africans, and East Asians several generations deep
in the United Kingdom. Night was scheduled to perform two shows in
one night at a club in central Birmingham, a place that Al guaranteed
would explode the minute that the singer hit the stage.

On the two-hour bus ride up the M1 motorway to Birmingham,

Night read the book *Twelve Years a Slave,* while Al and the band traded stories about their favorite tours. D listened and laughed at the tales, his attention sometimes caught by texts from Kira documenting her own car ride to Birmingham to hook up with them. She vowed she was "finally going to show all of you how to party properly" up north.

"Yo," Night said, as he saw D peering down at his BlackBerry, "you getting strung out on Kira?"

"No, but I'd be lying if I said she didn't have me a little open."

"Long-distance love is sweet," Night said. "I've had a lot of it. A short-term thing can stretch out when it's across the pond, you know."

"Enjoy it while it lasts, right?"

"That's true of everything, D. Shit, I'm trying to remember that myself. I love the love I'm getting. I let it go for too long. But whatever, you know? I'm enjoying this right now. Right this moment. How long that'll last?" Night shrugged.

"You are back, Night," D said reassuringly. "You are here to stay."

"D, you know I came from hustling. I did plenty of dirt. I had sex with a lot of people I didn't give a fuck about and who didn't give a fuck about me. Singing saved me from that. But whatever I had wrong with me before I got a record deal, it didn't just go away. I did rehab. A few times, you know. I take pills for my mood and shit. I'm doing all right. But I ain't really safe. I ain't safe from myself."

"Who is?"

"Yup . . . So Kira," Night said, "just let it do what it do."

It was dark when they reached Birmingham, which was fine since its central area was mostly nondescript government structures and low-rent shopping strips with some old buildings maintained for a hint of tradition. The club was bigger than Ronnie Scott's but lacked the London venue's historic pedigree.

The audience was as multicultural as Al had advertised, with D feeling like they were in DC or Atlanta. He had no idea what ethnic mix was in the house but the crowd was beautiful in a medley of browns, beiges, and yellows. Night, excited by all that loveliness, sang with a reckless abandon he hadn't reached in London. The crush at the backstage door after the show was intense and Night befriended a statuesque Nigerian beauty queen named Osas who rode back with them to London later that same night.

It wasn't until they were pulling away from Birmingham that D realized he hadn't seen Kira or any of her posse. A woman like that, D mused, could be anywhere doing anything.

There was a heavy knock on his door around noon the next day. D pushed through his persistent jet lag, yawned heavily, and tried to stretch out the cramps from the ride back from Birmingham. Al, Pilgrim, and a wet-eyed Night stood outside his door.

"What's up, gents?"

"Kira is dead," Al said flatly.

D sighed so deeply that for a moment he wasn't sure he could inhale again. He felt as if his breath was indefinitely suspended and might never come back. His body slumped and then sagged so that he found himself on the floor of the hallway, sitting there like a little child who'd lost his toys, crying, feeling silly and defeated. *No love in this world for me,* he thought. *No love.* It was an ugly notion but it was the only one he had.

The other men picked him up and laid him on the same bed he'd made love to Kira on little more than twenty-four hours earlier. Though the room had been cleaned since then, D could still smell that sexy woman—her perfume, her sweat, her breath. Like life itself, the scents were tart and sharp, sexy and sugary, and together just bittersweet.

They delayed the flight home two days so that Night could sing "Amazing Grace" at Kira's funeral. It was a very traditional Presbyterian service at a small chapel in Dalston. Her family was as respectable and prim as Kira had been cocky and fly. Her chubby mom and rail-thin dad didn't look like the parents of such a butterfly, though bits of Kira's loveliness shone through their very sad eyes.

Much of the church was filled with vampires from Kira's nightlife world, who'd risen from their daylight graves to see her buried in a permanent one. The casket was closed. Her luminous features had been crushed when her car flipped over an M1 divider about thirty minutes outside of Birmingham. The investigation was still underway but the alcohol level in her blood had been far too high. A gorgeous portrait of her dressed in a tidy school uniform stood near the coffin. D felt her eyes on him and winked back.

On the long, quiet flight home D contemplated how life creeped by and no matter how high you got, you died and they died, and you had to be good with it. That was it. Nothing else.

Someone tapped him on his shoulder. "You awake?" It was Night, looking boyishly excited.

"Kinda. You seem happy."

"Come with me to the restroom."

"Mile-high club, my dude? I'm flattered."

"Just come on, nigga."

The two men huddled by the business-class restroom as a very pretty flight attendant came out, smiled demurely at them, and walked away.

Night stuck his head inside the stall, hummed sweetly, and said, "Good echo right here."

"Yeah, it sounds like a project staircase."

"So I was thinking about Kira. It ain't a love song but, I dunno, this is what came out." Night began singing very quietly.

They burned my wings
They tore at my soul
I gasped a last breath
And I fell way down
But my will is strong
My faith is in this song
Watch me fly
Baby, I'm a phoenix . . .

I cannot stop
Baby, I'm a phoenix
Wind at my back
Baby, I'm a phoenix . . .

Rise with me, lovers
Rise with me, brothers
These chains will fall away
We'll be triumphant today
Hey, I'm a phoenix
Baby, I'm a phoenix . . .

I've been stung
I've been hung
Been left for dead and spit upon
I've bowed my head in shame
I've cried like a baby in the rain

But I would not stop
My belief in me too strong
Baby, I'm a phoenix
I can still play my love
Baby, I'm a phoenix . . .

"Damn," D said, "sounds very Sam Cooke. Curtis Mayfield too."

"Glad you like it. Not a hit single but I'm feeling it. And I'm so happy you been here with me. It just really helped me stay centered and shit."

"*And shit.* There's always something."

"Yeah . . . So we got this US tour coming up," Night said nervously. "My first time around the country in a long time. I'd really like you out there with me. It'll just be clubs."

"I dunno. Pilgrim and me got some bad history."

"I heard, but that's got nothing to do with you and me. Besides, you need me too, one-letter-name man."

D laughed. "You probably right."

"Are you gonna sing again?" It was the flight attendant, standing there with her arms folded over her red blazer and white blouse. D couldn't tell if she was mixed or Middle Eastern or what, but whatever her nationality, she was cute and knew it.

"Did I bother any of the folks sleeping?"

"I'm sure you did," she said, "but I want to hear more. My name is Bibi, by the way."

The two men introduced themselves and then D, a vet of such musician-meets-fan encounters, excused himself. From his seat he saw the two disappear into the toilet stall, and a moment later he heard Night's voice, crooning so sweet, and then laughter. D closed his eyes and embraced sleep.

TIGHTROPE

Stabs of anxiety ran through D, like a knife in and out of his gut. He'd sleep thirty or forty minutes, then roll back into consciousness. 2:49 a.m. 3:14 a.m. 4:09 a.m. There was no rest in this slumber. It felt like he'd been lifting boulders; his shoulders and neck ached. It felt like the flu, but was more likely dread.

D was waiting for a knockout punch. Instead he just found himself being pummeled. A fleet little man with hands of stone was pounding his kidneys, ribs, stomach to putty. At 4:45 a.m. D gave up and sat on the side of his bed like James Brown in a cold sweat. If he'd screamed it would have been as passionately piercing anything from the Godfather himself.

D walked over to his window. He was back in Brooklyn. It had been two days since he'd landed at JFK, but his body was still on UK time. His view was nothing special—an alley and an ancient air shaft. But a breeze came in. He could hear a couple fucking or fighting or both somewhere upstairs, which strangely calmed him down. D pulled out his iPod, his Beats by Dre headphones, and sat on his sofa and went to his neosoul song list, playing Maxwell and Badu and D'Angelo and Jill Scott and Night as the sky slowly lightened and his mind drifted.

London had been a respite, sexy and grim by turns, and it was still very much on D's mind as he ambled along in the early-evening darkness along Eastern Parkway. After stopping in front of the Botanic Garden, he was about to count off ten paces when he felt eyes on him. Not the causal gaze of a dog walker or of a passing driver, but the intense eyes of someone for whom D's body was, at that moment, the center of the universe.

D turned around slowly, moving past the Brooklyn Museum toward Franklin Avenue and its hipster enclave. Lots of bars, restaurants, and brightly lit gourmet grocery stores now lined the area north of Eastern Parkway, creating a mini-Williamsburg.

D strolled down Franklin and then turned into Franklin Park. He headed through the corridor into a long, high-ceilinged bar. He ordered a Bud Lite and sat in the patio, positioning himself so he could see both the entrance to the corridor and the establishment's back door.

The crowd was twentyish and dotted with bearded men, tattooed women, and had a general air of frivolity. Franklin Park was definitely a New Brooklyn spot but D wasn't feeling judgmental. Though born and raised in the borough, D had spent so much time away that he didn't feel entitled to look down on its new residents. In a way, D was an intruder too. At least he'd been feeling that way since his "homecoming." So he sat amongst his fellow newbies, wondering if maybe it was just new-to-Brooklyn paranoia that had him sitting there anxiously.

Before long he noticed a young black man at the bar in a flat-brimmed baseball cap with the word ASYA written in block letters. His pants were narrow and hung slightly off his ass. His high-top sneakers were a garish mix of black, yellow, aqua, and white. D recognized him as one of the guys outside the ARoc office, but he'd been the one who laid back and calmed the commotion.

This kid wasn't a thug but he definitely knew a few. D decided to wait and see who else showed up. He was finishing his second beer and munching on pretzels when, from the narrow corridor, in came

Asya Roc, strutting like he was in total control even while looking completely out of place. His homeboy nodded in D's direction and the rap star bopped over. D was at a loss, trying to take in the many layers of clothing draped upon the skinny young man's body. Highlights included gold Nikes with wings, a flat-brimmed cap with his name written across in Gothic letters, and a T-shirt featuring Pam Grier in bodacious Foxy Brown mode. There was a vest in the mix, a couple of chains, and tats popping off sections of exposed flesh.

"You have more ink than when I last saw you," D said.

"Yeah," Asya responded warily, "they got mad talent over in Europe. Got all these new tats on my arm right here." He pulled up a sleeve to reveal his shoulder, where an image of Ron O'Neal as Super Fly in a wide-brimmed hat, a long coat, mutton-chop sideburns, and the whole blaxploitation nine. "I'ma bring that era back. Wait until you see my next video. Long coats. Sideburns. Electra 225s."

"Nice," D said and nodded, acting impressed as Asya took a seat across from him. "So, I had a run-in with some dudes who claimed to represent you."

"They my peeps, no doubt. Hope they didn't rough you up too much."

"It didn't get to that. Your friend over there helped chill things out."

"Yo, Ree is my boy from way back. He keeps his head on straight."

"So do I."

"I see that. I didn't get what you were doing that night. I got worried. Thought maybe you were gonna try to blackmail me."

"That's not how I roll."

"Like I said, I see. No one seems to really know about the delivery who doesn't need to know about you. I respect that."

"So," D asked, "what are you gonna tell the police?"

"Niggas tried to rob me. You dragged me out. I bounced. Had a plane to catch. That's all."

"And the delivery?"

"If anyone saw shit, it was you carrying a bag that you left with. Feel me?"

"So we're good?"

"All that official shit will be good. But I paid for a delivery and I'm willing to pay more to get it back."

"You can dead that idea," D said. "The items are gone. I wanted you to know that. Face-to-face. They're gone. Won't be coming back."

Asya sat back in his chair and stared at D, anger and disbelief communicated with a smirk. He glanced over to his pal who, as if tugged by an invisible cord, got pulled into his orbit.

"Is there a problem, A?" Ree asked upon arrival.

For a hip hop hanger-on, this young man's delivery was surprisingly refined and calm. Not what D had expected. Asya explained the situation to Ree, who listened silently and then said, "Move over."

The star shifted docilely to make space.

"We haven't been formally introduced." The kid reached his hand across the table. "D, my name is Ree. I'm A's partner. Most people don't know me cause I play the background. Now, I need to know something—have you really tossed the guns away or are you holding them until you figure out when you gonna blackmail us?"

"Neither," D answered. "As I told Asya, I'm not gonna blackmail you. But I haven't tossed them in the river yet either."

"You just closed your office," Ree said. "Your business is falling apart. Why should we believe you won't come at us for some dough?"

"Why do you want *those* guns? There are a lot of them out there."

"We paid for them. We want them," Ree said.

"That's it?"

"That's it."

"Okay," D said, "are you close to Ice?"

"We know of him."

"Well, speak to him or one of his people and they'll let you know I'm legit."

Then Asya asked, "You know a nigga named Ray Ray from Tilden?"

"Yeah. He works for me sometimes."

"Okay," Ree said, "I know him. He's been trying to get in the rap game with us. He has some decent beats." Then he got up, took out his phone, and walked away from the table, leaving in his wake an awkward silence.

D broke it by saying, "I heard you turned out Birmingham."

"We did it big, yo. I had no idea it was gonna be like that. The women up there were crazy. You hit that with Night, right?"

"Yeah. He loved it too. Did you meet a woman named Kira?"

"Oh hell yeah, I did. Her crew were all dimes. She rolled with us back to London and I don't think we slept that night."

"She's dead."

"What?"

"Just last week, in a car accident riding between London and Birmingham."

The little boy who resided behind the gear and inside the rap star popped out. "Oh damn, that's crazy. That's so crazy." And then he fell silent, staring into space, eyes empty.

Asya was still off in his own London memories when Ree sat back down and said to his partner, "Remember that story about the brothers who got killed over on Mother Gaston? Well, this is the one who lived."

"Yo," Asya said, "you the one they tell stories about? Three dead brothers, right?"

D nodded calmly but inside was upset that Ray Ray had told Ree his sad history. He was also surprised at how fascinated these two young men were with it.

"My uncle told me about your family. Lots of people know that story. They all got murked on Rockaway Avenue."

"It was on the corner of Livonia and Stone, or what they call Mother Gaston now," D said.

Asya sat back and gazed at D with new eyes. "You that nigga. You the survivor. I'm gonna write a song called 'The Survivor' based on your story. If I'd known all this we wouldn't have had no kind of misunderstanding. Right, Ree?"

"D, you are a real B-Ville homey," Ree said slowly. "So I don't feel like I got to worry about you."

"You don't," D assured him.

"But there were people who had plans for those guns. It's got nothing to do with us now cause we don't have them and we are no longer involved. But we can't call them off either."

"Does this involve a Detective Rivera?"

Ree smiled. "Yo, you don't snitch, right? Same thing over here."

"There's such a thing as dry snitching," D said.

Ree and Asya exchanged a look and then turned back toward D. "He's a force out there," Ree said, and considered his next words carefully. "There's this real estate company that's moving into Brownsville called AKBK. Detective Rivera is doing some private security for them. I hear they have big plans for the Ville. You should check them out."

"This is connected to the delivery?"

"Like he said, you should look into that, yo," Asya chimed in. "You and your pal Ice."

"So we were being set up. No—Ice was being set up?"

"D," Ree said, "that's as dry as I can be. We good on that now, okay? So could you tell Asya a bit about what happened to your brothers? If you help us there may be a ways we could give you a piece of the song. What you say, Asya?"

"That could happen," the MC replied.

So, in the spirit of making potential enemies into collaborators, clients into comrades, D shared the bloody tale of his family while calculating the connection between Rivera, Ice, and AKBK Realty.

Ask of You

"I have a lead for you."

D was coming up Flatbush from the Barclays Center where he'd just purchased a couple of Brooklyn Nets caps—one white, one black—and the windbreaker he was already wearing which fit real nice. His good mood was broken by the older man's tired voice.

"That's nice," D said as he entered Woodland and eyeballed a lovely dark-brown woman with woolly natural hair. He gave her a big smile as she handed him a menu. "I was wondering if our employer was just donating to his favorite African American charity or really wanted us to find this vinyl."

"Archer is generous," Edge said through the BlackBerry, "but not *that* generous. He'd like some results."

"Good. What's the lead?"

"You heard of this tech businesswoman Faith Newman?"

"Don't know her." D sat down at a table by a window facing out onto Sixth Avenue and watched the slender hostess stride back to her station.

"I'm seventy-one," Edge said, "and I know who she is."

"I don't watch reality shows."

"I do. But that's not why you should know her. She's one of them Internet billionaire types. You know who Mark Cuban is?"

"The guy who owns the Mavs."

"Faith Newman is Mark Cuban with a pussy."

"That's a highly unappetizing visual, my friend."

"I agree, but I see you finally get it. She made a grip by selling a company that helped retailers do inventory better. At least that's what I read in *Forbes* magazine."

"This woman is a record collector?"

"More than that," Edge said. "She's a wannabe vocalist. Apparently she's working on an LP. Sees herself as a sophisticated soul singer. Has idolized Diana Ross, Donna Summer, and various divas since she was a kid."

"She sounds like a gay man. Anyway, you're saying she got herself a rare Diana Ross record because she loves La Ross? Okay. This lead . . . is it based on any real information?"

"How would I know?" Edge said. "Motherfucker is paying us to ask some questions. So let's ask some questions."

"Hey, is there some kind of deadline on this search?"

"You got something else to do?"

"Lots," D replied.

"Anything paying like this?"

"No."

"When you find a better gig let me know, cause I'd like another one too."

"How's your health, Edge?"

"I'm okay, except I could use new hips, a revamped heart, and about 50 percent less sugar in my blood. Thanks for asking."

"Once we find this record, or once he gets tired of us looking, what are your plans?"

"I got no plans." The old man sounded amused by the thought. "My previous plan was to eat unhealthy, drink a lot, and find a willing woman too young for me."

"That's not a plan. That's just bad behavior."

"Maybe," Edge said, no longer amused. "Listen, no rush on this, but just don't do nothing. You feel me?"

"Gotcha. But how do I get a billionaire lady to talk to me?"

"Stay tuned," the old man said, and clicked off.

A lean, bohemian black man, wearing a colorful wool cap on his head and black frames on his face, entered, walked over to the hostess D had been watching, and kissed her.

He'd eaten a salad and was finishing his grilled chicken when an e-mail buzzed on his BlackBerry. It was Faith Newman's office inquiring if D was available to meet the next day at four p.m.

I'm Coming Out

D had expected the big corporate runaround. Lots of waiting and then filling out paperwork for some grim-faced drone across a desk in a room with harsh lighting in a building somewhere in Manhattan. Instead, he found himself way out in deep Bushwick, a place this native Brooklynite had rarely visited. In his mind, Bushwick was a hood filled with Puerto Ricans, cheap frame houses, and decaying factory buildings.

The town car rolled north on Bedford from Prospect Heights and made a right on Flushing, passing through another large Hassidic enclave that gave way to the elevated subway on Broadway and an area that still reflected D's old-school vision of the hood (Latin takeout, kids in hoodies, public housing) before shifting to warehouses converted into lofts.

The new white residents of Bushwick, most in their late twenties and early thirties, were strolling around, looking more authentically hipster than the folks who now resided in Williamsburg. D saw yoga studios and art galleries, rental trucks unloading film equipment, and pedestrians clutching Samsung smartphones like reunited lovers.

D was dropped off across the street from a nondescript gray four-story building with a gourmet coffee shop on the ground floor. He thought it looked like home base to roomy artists' lofts but not necessarily the office of a multibillion-dollar operation.

He pressed the third-floor buzzer by the steel door where a tab read, *Nightbirds*, the name of Labelle's classic 1974 LP. A camera light flashed on, a computerized voice asked his name, he replied, and the door opened. A man with a buzz cut, goatee, and a heavyweight's build sat on a stool behind a table with a tablet and phone on top. He wore a tight-fitting blue vintage blazer and a lovely beige shirt. On the wall behind him was a blowup of the cover of *Nightbirds*. He looked up and said, "You're good. The elevator's out, so use the stairs."

The staircase was worn, but not dirty, with old-school R&B posters hanging in frames that had been artfully distressed. The Shirelles at the Apollo. Labelle headlining the Met. Diana Ross & the Supremes at the Copacabana. Diana Ross at Radio City. The acts on the wall were all female and the posters grew more gaudy with each ensuing decade. Plus, there were cameras everywhere.

On the third-floor landing there was a psychedelic Eyrkah Badu poster near a stylized black, white, and red image of Janelle Monáe. Another door read, *Nightbirds,* and D passed through it into a long room with walls painted a warm rust color, the ceiling a vibrant azure—the colors of a Mumbai alley, not a Bushwick loft.

The staff was standard-issue yuppified twenty-first-century hipster, though clearly there was someone in management with a very particular sensibility. Manjit, a dark Indian woman with a highly professional smile, offered him bottled water and a seat on an old-school park bench painted emerald green. D sat there for about fifteen minutes before Manjit reappeared and escorted him past rows of folks at computers to an office with a pane of frozen glass facing the larger room.

On the other side of the glass was a large space with the same color scheme as the outer office but furnished like a living room. Coffee table, jars of nuts and candy, an old Motorola hi-fi. From this side of the glass you gazed at all the tech minions toiling in a nicely appointed digital sweatshop.

Sitting on a long comfy sofa along the wall facing Flushing Avenue was Faith Newman, a stocky blonde dressed like a *Girls* extra save her rather glamorous, bejeweled Wayfarer glasses. It was a touch of excess that made D think the dour outfit that surrounded it was actually a costume and the glasses revealed who Faith really was (or wanted to be).

"D Hunter," she said, standing up, "so glad you could take the time to come meet with me."

He'd never had a billionaire kiss his ass before. "If you say so," he replied with a smile. "I'd say it was the other way around."

She guided him to a seat on the sofa. D found Faith's iridescent frames distracting. "You just came off tour with Night. How is he sounding these days?"

"Very strong. Probably not exactly as you might remember him. He's evolved."

"But still soulful?"

"Very soulful."

"I saw him seven or eight times back when his first album came out," she said pleasantly.

"Whoa, you are a very serious fan."

"*Very* serious. I love R&B."

"The walk up the stairway is like an R&B history lesson," he said.

"You were friends with the historian Dwayne Robinson, weren't you?"

"Yeah," he said, surprised. "He was a real mentor to me."

"I have autographed copies of all his books. *The Relentless Beat* is like my Bible. Believe me, I'd rather have been Stevie Wonder than Bill Gates."

D chuckled, not sure if she was being patronizing or not. He waited for her next move, which was: "So, what happened with your company?"

"We had a good run," he said, feeling a bit anxious. "But when the record business went south, a lot of my usual vendors—record labels, managers—had to cut their budgets. And the business that remained just got silly. So many of the youngsters that pass for rap stars these days—well, they and their friends are reckless, and reckless can lead to bloodshed. It's one thing to want to be secure. Its another to walk into fire using gasoline for cologne."

"You talk like a songwriter, D."

"Ha, maybe in a previous life," D said, slightly flattered. "In this one I'm just a big man with big hands. If there was music in these fingers it got beat out of them years ago."

"Have you beaten many people, D?"

"No," he answered firmly, then added, "but I have grabbed a few folks and shook the hell out of them."

"Are you always this funny?"

"I wish. Job interviews make me nervous. I probably say too much."

"No. You are doing fine. The truth is, I don't need more security. I have a very expensive company on retainer. But whenever Michael Archer sends me a recommendation I take it seriously. I looked at your résumé and saw you had a long professional relationship with someone I want to do business with."

"You want me to help you in business? Okay, how could I possibly do that?"

"I want you to introduce me to Night."

"That's it? Meeting Night?"

"Can you arrange that?"

"I think so. I know you sing and write songs. He'll want to hear some of your music first."

An anxious expression filled her face. "Oh, don't tell him I want to meet about my music. No. Tell him it's about helping him build up his social network and online presence. I'd be embarrassed to have him hear me sing. I'm not ready for that."

"So you wanna meet under false pretenses?" D suddenly felt in control.

"No. I mean I can help him in a number of ways. I'm definitely a fan."

"Maybe one day you'll do a duet."

"Please do not condescend to me. I don't respond well to that."

"That wasn't my intention."

"Whatever your intention, that was the effect." Faith Newman clearly had an edge and D's comment made her flash the blade.

"Won't happen again. So, should I hit your secretary when I have it hooked up with Night?"

"No. Text me directly." Faith pulled out a futuristic-looking device and sent him her number.

"Cool. By the way, do you have a big record collection?"

Faith seemed amused by his question. "Not really. As you can see, I have a pretty extensive collection of soul and R&B posters. But actual vinyl? What you see over there," she pointed to her vintage turntable, "is what I have, and those are gifts from Michael Archer."

D took a quick look at the vinyl. Two Diana Ross & the Supremes albums from the '60s, the Ike & Tina Turner album that contained the Phil Spector produced "River Deep–Mountain High," and a pristine copy of Labelle's *Nightbirds* album. "All my music is digital these days. Does Michael have you searching out some obscure, super-rare soul single?"

"Yeah, he said he thought you had it."

Faith laughed. "Silly man. He knows better than that. I guess he just wanted us to meet."

"He has feelings for you?"

The woman just shook her head like this was a tired old story. "Did you see his castle?"

"Yes, I had the pleasure."

"Well that's not me," she said firmly. "I love the past but adore the present. Michael knows my affection for Night, D. So here you are." She reached out and shook his hand. "I will be grateful if you make this happen. Incidentally, I'm hosting a benefit for a new Brooklyn charity my boyfriend and I are involved with. Please come as my guest. I will send you the details."

D was back out on Flushing Avenue when his BlackBerry buzzed and an e-mail from Nightbirds arrived with an attachment. It was a benefit for Grow Brooklyn, a charity that he'd never heard of. One of the sponsors was AKBK Realty. Obviously a party not to be missed.

LOVE HANGOVER

Back in Brownsville again. In his old hood more in this past month than in decades. He sat again in the McDonald's, a place he detested, to meet with a man lost in his memories. D understood the feeling. Though it was only a short walk away, D wouldn't set foot on the corner of Livonia and Mother Gaston. His reluctance made him feel like a punk, but that fear in his gut couldn't be pushed away. It felt DNA deep.

He sat sucking on the ice at the bottom of his Coke cup, cursing his timidity, when a shadow crossed the table and Ride sat down.

"Looks like you found my girl," he said.

"That's her, huh?"

"And that was me in the photo," he confirmed.

"So," D asked gingerly, "have you hit her on Facebook?"

"I did. A couple of other folks I know on Facebook did too."

"And?"

"And she didn't respond. Then she shut down her Facebook page."

"I take it Eva doesn't want to be in contact with you."

Ride stared out the window. "Damn bitch," he said under his breath.

"Is she afraid of you?"

Ride peered at D and the bodyguard tensed his body, thinking the bigger man might swing at him. "She shouldn't be," Ride growled.

"But it seems like she does."

"I left some money with her. Looks like she used it to move to Los Angeles. That was her plan for us. Guess she couldn't wait for me."

"What now, Ride?"

"Gotta get out West. Not right away though . . ." His voice trailed off. "I like that kid Ray Ray. He's smart. Has some heart."

D shook his head. "Maybe too much."

"You can never have too much heart," Ride countered. "People gonna chip away at it every day. You need as much as you can get. Speaking of which, I hear you have a problem with some people."

"What have you heard?"

"That there was a shooting scenario and you were a witness, and that some people are nervous you'll implicate someone's meal ticket. That sound close?"

"Real close."

"I imagine this must be on your mind a lot. Must worry you having that kind of pressure."

"You know the hood cats who stepped to me?"

"These youngsters don't know how to keep their traps shut. Cops don't need to go undercover anymore. They just go on YouTube and decide what felony they wanna prosecute a nigga for. Truth be told, I know some heads. I can speak to a few for you."

"That's not necessary."

"No. I see you, D. I see what you're about. I didn't give you a lot to work with but you came through for me. Now that I'm out, I'm seeing how things work. It's a different world. Brooklyn's different."

"No question about that," D agreed.

"So D, I need a job."

"I don't follow you."

"I need a job. Something to tell my PO. Something to tell my mother.

She's worried that I'm gonna re-up for incarceration. Me and my cousin both."

"Do I know him?"

"He was the guy you saw watching me the other day."

"You were real mysterious about who he was."

"I know. It feels like a pussy move to have him shadowing me, but Mom Dukes has him reporting back to her."

"He's a human ankle bracelet."

They both laughed, relaxing into an unexpected camaraderie.

"Shit yeah," Ride said. "But after all that time in jail, I'm used to being watched. So let me know what you can do. I'll get back to you about that shooting scenario."

"Ride, if my security company was doing better, I'd give you a shot in a heartbeat. If anything comes my way, I got you."

Ride stood and embraced D. As the ex-con walked away, D realized he had a new friend.

BE HERE

Wythe Avenue, between North 11th and 12th streets, had become a central intersection for Brooklyn's burgeoning nightlife. On the corner of 11th was the Wythe Hotel, which sported a brilliant red neon sign that could be seen for miles and a rooftop bar that offered a grand view of Manhattan's skyline. Across the street in the middle of the block was Brooklyn Bowl, a bowling alley/restaurant/concert venue that had become a steady home for jam bands, alternative hip hop acts, and the Roots's Ahmir "Questlove" Thompson who DJ'ed a Thursday-night party. On the corner of North 12th, on the same side as the Wythe Hotel, was Output, where hip hop legend Q-Tip mixed funk and hip hop classics Wednesdays in the main room.

But on this Tuesday night the hotel and the two clubs were all supporting the Grow Brooklyn fundraiser that was the brainchild of D's new pal Faith Newman. A $200 ticket gave you access to all three venues where Questlove, Q-Tip, and a slew of other top DJs were spinning. At both ends of Wythe there were checkpoints where revelers were given orange wristbands. Though the crowd was largely white, there was a healthy number of blacks, Latinos, and Asians in the mix as well.

Remarkable, at least to D, was that he wasn't doing security. Instead he sat in Output's VIP section, nodding his head to Q-Tip rocking the packed house with a lively '80s hip hop set. Faith had insisted he "chill" with her, though the tech lady and her boyfriend were far from cool.

"Ownership is everything to me," Faith said, standing uneasily on high heels with a half-filled glass of vodka in her hand. "I mean ownership of the precious. Scarcity is truly regal. It's almost spiritual."

D gazed at this superrich woman and then down at the blocky beige, expensive shoes she wobbled in, and wondered if she was destined to keel over and into his lap. Her boyfriend, a goateed, petite, and handsome young white guy named Cassidy Ronson, sat curled up in a fetal position on the banquette, his eyes focused on the backlit bottle of vodka on the table before him. Ronson hadn't spoken in fifteen minutes. D had long been amused at the party habits of the webistocracy, a group who desperately wanted to out-ball Diddy, but didn't have the constitution.

Ronson had something more potent than vodka in his system, which he seemed to be enjoying, but Faith was determined to make him sociable. She bent down and shook her boyfriend who sat upright and worked to focus his eyes.

"Cassidy, D here grew up in Brownsville."

"Oh," he responded. "I have an office there."

"Really? What are you doing in Brownsville?"

"I have controlling interest in a company called AKBK Realty."

D stared at this high-ass hipster and his eyes almost popped out of his head. Hard for him to believe this little man was somehow involved in Rivera's mess, but here he was. "You guys are on Livonia Avenue, right?" he said as innocently as possible. "I grew up in the Tilden projects just a few blocks away."

The mention of public housing sent a jolt through Ronson's body. "That part of Brooklyn has been so poorly served by government planners," he said excitedly.

"That would be what you'd call an understatement," D replied.

"You might not know this, but one of the culprits was a French design theorist named Le Corbusier."

"He worked out of Washington?"

"No, no," Ronson spoke rapidly. "But he impacted the thinking of planners in DC and around the world in the '50s and '60s. Robert Moses fell in love with his work. Le Corbusier argued that the way to create democratic working-class housing was to construct high-rise structures that were very uniform in nature. So it was a top-down idea that spread around the world, from the suburbs of France to India to the Tilden projects where you grew up. The city planners of the period, influenced by Le Corbusier, never involved the future residents in the design process. They just built these tall sterile buildings and then poured people into preplanned structures and told them to behave. Le Corbusier believed form trumped any traditions or cultural differences."

"That didn't quite work out," D said, struggling to seem engaged.

"No, it did not. But Moses and the other city planners didn't end their folly with the Tilden or Van Dyck housing developments. Right down the street from my office they built the Marcus Garvey development."

"Know it well."

"Marcus Garvey was designed as the anti–Le Corbusier. An architect named Oscar Newman wrote a book called *Creating Defensible Space* which argued for low-rise, individual entrances with little stoops. Only 625 apartments. Instead of large public spaces in front where anyone could walk through, he envisioned connected minibackyards that kept outsiders out and created—"

"Drug dealer central." This was history D knew very well. "Folk Nation and some other gangs made that home."

"Cut off from prying eyes, those interconnected backyards were a haven for crack sales. All the things that the planners thought would make Marcus Garvey superior to Tilden and other high-rise developments actually made it worse."

"So you guys are gonna do a better job than the government?"

"We certainly hope so. Couldn't do worse, right? As a person raised in this community, you would know how desperate life can be out here."

"I appreciate the history, Cassidy. I lived a lot of it. But you own this AKBK Realty so you must have a plan."

Now Ronson's rhythm slowed and he began picking his words carefully. "Well, Mr. Hunter, that's still evolving. If you look at the demographic patterns in Brooklyn you'll see that Brownsville is no longer only African American. On Pitkin you've had a significant influx of West African merchants. There's a growing Asian community in the western part of Brownsville. When you look at what's happening in East Bushwick with postcollege whites and the artist community there, you see that Brownsville's future is, like all of New York, about change."

D poked gently for more: "But what about the projects? You think people are gonna have chai lattes across from those ghettos in the sky?"

"Do you still spend time out there?" Ronson replied.

"I have some old friends and clients there," D said neutrally.

"What's up, D?" Night, looking healthy and accompanied by a stunning young model named Porsche, had just arrived. Faith Newman hopped off the banquette, smoothed out her dress, and smiled beatifically. D gave Night a hug and quickly introduced the singer to the tech mogul and her ghetto real estate–speculating boyfriend. Quickly Ronson and Faith cornered Night, speak-shouting into his ear as D watched from a few feet away. He'd gotten a reluctant Night to come out to this benefit by promising to go on the road with him despite the presence of Amos Pilgrim.

Time passed. D chatted with Porsche and thought about that re-

ceptionist at ARoc, wondering why he hadn't invited her. D was dancing with the model when Ronson, looking increasingly wired, tapped
him on the shoulder.

"This is my card," he said. "Let's meet tomorrow about the concert."

"The concert?"

"Yeah. The free show Night is gonna play for Grow Brooklyn at
Betsy Head Park in Brownsville."

D headed over to Night, who was sitting at the VIP table while Faith
danced on top of the banquette next to him. The singer was chuckling
and taking quick peeks up the woman's dress.

"You gonna do this?" D asked.

"It's your hood, right?"

"But you haven't done a show in New York in years. Don't you
wanna speak with Pilgrim?"

"Faith just talked to him. She guaranteed X amount of dollars. You
handle the arrangements." Then Night laughed and said, "I'm gonna
make a manager out of you, D."

LONELY TEARDROPS

Junior's had never been D's favorite restaurant. He of course loved the cheesecake though otherwise wasn't a fan of their kitchen. But Edge had wanted to eat there and was picking up the check, so here he was at the downtown Brooklyn institution, sitting under a painting of the Brooklyn Dodgers's sainted Ebbets Field. The place was gonna close soon and be torn down to build the latest Brooklyn condo, but D didn't have the heart to tell Edge the bad news.

"I have some news for you," Edge said after he settled into the booth. "I'm out."

"What do you mean *out?* Out of what?"

"I'm leaving New York. I just got a gig that's gonna take me down South, and once I get there I'm staying."

"I thought the Englishman was paying you to find that record," D said.

"Well, you met him. Archer liked you and decided to let me go."

"What? He liked *me?* That man talked to me like a servant."

"And you gave as good as you got. At least that's his story. He respected that. So you'll deal with him directly from now on."

"I dunno," D said.

"I do. I got his last check in my pocket. With that money and the new gig, I'm ready to settle down South."

"What kind of job does your old ass have?"

"I'm gonna hit the road from New York to Florida with some young rapper. Gonna take him to radio and clubs along the way."

"That's a job for a kid, not an AARP member."

Edge chuckled. "Flattery will get you nowhere. One of the last re-maining black record executives owed me a favor, so he threw me a bone. I can't go back to that seniors' home in the Bronx. Can't happen. I was gonna be dead up there in a year. That arrogant-ass Englishman gave me a new lease on life. Now I'm buying the property."

"I'll miss you, Edge."

"If I stayed in this city any longer I was gonna miss myself. This city isn't made for poor people and it's got nothing to offer an old black man but sad memories and pity. Shit, barely a bar I liked in Harlem or Bed-Stuy that ain't gone or started selling Italian coffee."

"Yo!" It was Ray Ray, with a flat-brimmed black Nets hat and pants sliding off his ass, bounding up the aisle looking even more boyish than usual.

"You are way early," D said. "We're supposed to meet at three p.m."

"Sorry, D. I got a lift down here and I took it. Besides, I think you told me once that early was on time."

"Nothing wrong with a young man being early, D," Edge said. "That's as rare as a summer tan in January. It's a twenty-first-century miracle. Young man, my name is Edgecombe Lenox but my friends call me Edge."

Ray Ray introduced himself, and to D's surprise, the old man moved over and let him sit down.

"Where you from?" Edge asked.

"Like D, I'm from Brownsville. I'm not trying to stay there. I wanna see the world too. D has helped me get out a bit. I'm looking for more."

"Yeah," Edge said, "you gotta have a dream. When I first came to New York I didn't have a pot to piss in or a window to toss it out of. But I knew what I wanted and was willing to do what I had to do."

"I feel the same way, yo."

"It almost goes without saying. Without money there's no food and shelter, and without food and shelter there is no life. You can go without love a lot longer than you can go without food or shelter. But aside from making money, what are you into?"

"I like music," Ray Ray said. "I've been making beats and looking to get some MCs to spit over them."

"Does that idea make you happy?"

"Of course. I want people to hear my shit."

"You go to church?"

"Not really," Ray Ray responded, slightly embarrassed. "My moms takes me on Easter. Sometimes we go during Christmas when we're feeling like Santa was good to us, you know."

"The reason I ask is I was wondering if you had a spiritual practice," Edge said. "It's useful to have some kind of god in your life when your money ain't right."

"There are some Five Percenters in my building. I chop it up with them sometimes."

"You live in Medina, so I could see how that would interest you."

"You down with the Gods? A lot of old heads are into that shit."

"I have pursued knowledge of self my whole life," Edge said sagely. "Read a lot of the Koran. A lot of the Bible. When I read them I see what's similar. You don't have to believe in every part of a spiritual practice to get value out of it. Any system man creates has value, though man—and woman—will eventually fuck it up cause that's just what we do."

"What? You a philosopher or something like that?"

"No, man. I sold records for a living. Should have been a philosopher cause records are a business that's no longer in business."

"I got a friend that had two hundred thousand hits on YouTube for this beat he made. He hooked it up and got some cash for it. He made money on his music just like that." Ray Ray was schooling Edge on twenty-first-century YouTube economics. D was worried the old man would be offended but he seemed to be enjoying it.

"You may be right, Raymond—I assume that's the name your mother gave you?"

"Yeah," Ray Ray admitted reluctantly.

"Maybe there's new ways to earn from music, but I'm just too damn old to evolve."

"I don't know, Edge," D said. "You seem to be doing fine right now."

"Lemme ask you something, Raymond. You know who James Brown is, right?"

"Of course. The Godfather of Soul. Lots of crazy beats that have been sampled. Every now and then my moms plays one of his jams at home."

"But do you know who Jackie Wilson is?"

"Naw," Ray Ray said.

"Well, he was better than James Brown onstage."

"Oh yeah?"

D felt a history lesson coming on, though he wasn't sure if Ray Ray would be receptive. This could be fun or quite painful.

"They were both Golden Gloves boxers and had that good foot-work. They both did splits. Weren't afraid to get on the floor. Not spin-ning like hip hoppers but they would get on their knees to sell a song. Jackie was actually more flexible than Brown. That man could get on his knees in his suit and bend backward like he was doing the limbo. Could limbo like that Harry Belafonte."

Knowing that *limbo* and *Harry Belafonte* were references the young man might not get, D suggested, "You should show him some footage."

"There's film out there," Edge said. "Shit, I have a VHS somewhere with all Jackie's TV appearances. The man was bad. I mean everyone talks about Michael Jackson being influenced by James Brown. That's not even near the truth. The truth was Michael came out of Jackie, from his posture onstage, his leg movements and spins. I mean, it's not even a question."

"Edge," D said, trying not to sound too amused, "no one has a VHS player anymore."

"What's a VHS?" Ray Ray asked.

"Go to YouTube on your phone, Ray Ray, and type in *Jackie Wilson*," D said, ignoring the question.

While the young man tapped on his Samsung Galaxy, Edge defended his VHS ownership. "In fact, I have two of them bad boys in a basement somewhere. Shit, I used to give them to program directors as gifts. D, if you need one, I can hook you up."

Laughing, D said, "No thanks. You hold onto that."

Ray Ray offered his phone to Edge and asked, "Which one of these clips should I watch?"

The elder man slid on a pair of glasses, peered at the little screen, and selected a clip of Wilson performing "Lonely Teardrops" in black-and-white on some early '60s TV show. Ray Ray watched it, mildly bored until about a minute into the song when Wilson leaped off a platform, gracefully landing on his spread-eagled knees and then, without breaking a sweat, sliding up to his feet.

"He's smooth!" Ray Ray said.

"The smoothest, Raymond. Can I tell you a story?"

Ray Ray knew instinctively there was no refusing. Even the fact that he had to go take a leak would have to be ignored for the moment.

The youngster hadn't known either of his grandfathers and had only fleeting contact with older men. He was enjoying the attention. Edge even made the usually hated "Raymond" sound respectable.

D actually had some things he needed to do. He wanted to go back with Ray Ray to his apartment to look at some more footage of Rivera. Against his wishes, the kid had followed the detective a few more times. It was extremely dangerous, but what was done was done. Yet D had a bit of a plan developing, one that could hurt Rivera.

But he was in no rush right now. He had always enjoyed Edge's tales of R&B past, the kind of stories Dwayne Robinson used to tell him over drinks. He didn't think he'd heard this particular Jackie Wilson story and was looking forward to either some wisdom or chuckles, and hopefully both.

"When I was no older than you," Edge began, "I used to run errands at the Apollo. *Go get me a beer. Go get me some Parliaments or Kools.* Jackie was a star. Just about the biggest star a black man could be back then. But he was real regular with me. *Real* regular. So one day he was headlining a bill with a singer named Marv Johnson. Like Jackie he was from Detroit and had a couple of hits. Nothing that lasted but he had a little thing happening.

"Before the first show of the day, Jackie tells me to watch Marv Johnson and notice the mistake he makes every time. So I go stand in the wings. Marv is okay. He ain't James Brown or Jackie Wilson but he gets a nice ovation. I tell Jackie I don't see anything. Jackie laughs and says, *You see how Marv only sings to the pretty girls?* Okay, so I wanna know how the hell is that a mistake cause it sounds like a winning program to me.

"Jackie just says, *Watch who I sing to.* So he goes out there and is just Jackie Wilson. 'Baby Workout.' 'Lonely Teardrops.' 'To Be Loved.'

Dancing his ass off. Leaping to his knees. His process starts to loosen from the sweat. Shirt goes untied. The usual exciting shit he does. Then I see it: Jackie is at the edge of the stage and the girls have come down the aisle. They are screaming like he's about to start rubbing that mic stand between their thighs. They are pulling at his sharkskin suit and they are ripping buttons off his creamy white shirt—the man's clothing bill must have been goddamn enormous—and, like I said, I see it. Genius."

"Damn, what the fuck was it?" Ray Ray asked.

"Jackie is singing to the most unattractive woman on 125th Street. I mean he is eyeballing this woman like there was hundred-dollar bills stuck between her eyes. And she is ecstatic like she has been anointed and Jackie is the Lord. I mean this woman is all aflutter."

Ray Ray was skeptical. "Making an ugly bitch come is genius?"

Edge ignored the question. "After the show Jackie quizzes me. *Did you see? I said, Yes sir. I saw you didn't sing to the pretty women. By singing to the homely woman you made every woman in the room think they had a chance with you, not just the fine girls. And the fine girls, they respect you for that. They know they got a shot with Jackie but they like how you are generous.* Marv Johnson was just trying to line up a hot girl to take back to his hotel and everyone in the Apollo knew it. Either of you remember Marv Johnson?"

Both his listeners shook their heads.

"See, there was a science to what Jackie did. Cause and effect. Shit, it was *scientific*. It ain't just about singing. It ain't just about dancing. You do something to create an effect. People feel it. They might not even know in their front mind what's going on, but in the back of their head they feel it."

"So if I manage an artist I gotta get them to sing to the ugly women?"

Ray Ray had seen a hint of disapproval in Edge's eyes when he said *bitch*, so he was cleaning up his language.

"Or ugly men. It works both ways. What's good for the bitch is good for the bastard too."

Ray Ray and D laughed. Edge beamed. It had been awhile since he'd had the ears of two young listeners, particularly someone Ray Ray's age. He hadn't seen his grandkids in years. They lived down South and after his oldest son had deposited him in the elder-care facility in the Bronx six years earlier, it was like they were embarrassed to come see him. Until this lost-record opportunity came his way, Edge had felt like a buried treasure, as forgotten as the "Country Boy & City Girl" single he was supposed to be finding.

But on this afternoon, in this company, Edge felt valued. For him, the real lost treasure of R&B was his self-respect.

Gettin' in the Way

On the wall in Cassidy Ronson's office was a framed blowup of Alfred Kazin's *A Walker in the City*, the famed literary critic's memoir of growing up in Brownsville in the 1930s, a time when the area was a notorious Jewish ghetto. That, D assumed, was where the AK in AKBK came from. On the opposite wall hung a huge map of Brownsville and neighboring East New York with different pins representing, D guessed, real estate holdings and possible acquisitions.

Other than that the office was pretty bare. Some file cabinets. A cappuccino machine. Ronson sat behind an battered wooden desk with some papers scattered across it. Now as clear-eyed as he'd been buzzed at the charity event, Ronson wore a bow tie, black-framed glasses, and a white shirt with suspenders. He looked like a parody of a 1950s banker.

D sat there amazed at this turn of events. He'd almost been shot and/or stabbed on the pavement outside. He'd watched videos of Rivera selling guns he had stored somewhere in this space. Now he was sitting across from an Ivy League guy working out the details for a free concert in the same public park he'd spent countless hours in as a youth. It was sweet in a way, but D knew this conversation was probably not going to end smoothly.

They'd spoken for thirty minutes with Amos Pilgrim via Skype. Once he'd clicked off and they'd completed D's checklist, Ronson went into a spiel that seemed a sober continuation of his Output rant.

"Before they built all this public housing, Brownsville's tenements were filled with Jews from Eastern Europe," Ronson explained. "Change happens. Our company will be here when it happens. We'll *help* it happen. We'll be stakeholders here. You are a stakeholder too. Which is why this concert should be the first of many projects we work on out here together."

"Real estate is not my game," D said bluntly.

"It's about much more than real estate, D. We are talking with the city about building a large cultural center in Brownsville called the Brevoort, after the vaudeville house that was kind of Brooklyn's Apollo. It was on Bedford off Fulton Street. We are giving it a classic old-school name but it'll be a totally modern venue where Brownsville's musical future can be developed. That sound good to you?"

"Sure," D said, "if you can pull it off."

"We need men of respect to represent us as we create our plan for Brownsville's development. You are from the area, you've worked with many celebrities, and then you moved back to Brooklyn. It's a great narrative—you'd just have to do some presentations initially. As our plan develops you'd be included in what we do. We won't make the same mistakes that happened in the past."

"That all sounds great, Cassidy. By the way, doesn't a Detective Rivera work for you?"

"Detective Rivera has done security for us as we moved through the neighborhood. You see where our office is. We are right in the heart of it, so having Rivera around has been helpful. That shooting you might have read about happened right outside this door and Rivera was involved in that, keeping this office from being vandalized."

"Did he really?" D worked hard to suppress his amusement.

"You see we've been threatened. People have e-mailed us saying they are going to shoot me and my employees if I don't hire this person or that or don't pay a 'tax' for working in Brownsville. So having some-one as formidable as Rivera makes sense."

"Cassidy, you've offered me a role of some kind in a business that seems to have some very vague goals and you currently employ one of the most corrupt policemen in this community. Now that suggests to me one of two things: you are either using him to strong-arm or intimi-date people, or you are totally clueless about Rivera's methods. Either one of those things disturbs me."

"Do you have any proof about Rivera's corruption?"

"You are the third organization to do work in Brownsville in recent years that has hired Rivera as a security consultant."

"He comes highly recommended—"

"By the precinct captain."

"Yes."

"Those other ventures received similar threats when they moved into the area." D reached inside his jacket and pulled out two folded sheets of paper. "I bet the language in these other e-mails is very similar to those you received."

Ronson took the pages and looked them over. "These just sound like they were written by ignorant kids," he said.

"Rivera is in business with lots of young knuckleheads."

"This is hard for me to believe."

"You see the forwarding e-mail address on those pages. FlyTy@gmail? That's retired New York City detective Tyrone Williams, who spent fif-teen or so years walking these streets. He can provide you with more details about Rivera's stellar career."

"Rivera has one of the highest conviction rates of any detective in Brooklyn," Ronson said. "I've seen paperwork that proves this. Your friend may simply be jealous."

D stood and headed toward the door. "Check your e-mail. There you'll find a link to a Vimeo page which contains footage of Rivera moving around Brownsville. I think you'll see him differently. And if not, it'll be handled eventually."

"It sounds like I may have come across as naïve to you." Ronson stood up too. "I believe in what we're doing. We don't have a master plan. We are collecting real estate with an eye toward being adaptable and not imposing our will."

"Get back to me after you've really checked on Rivera, and when I say *checked*, I don't mean talking to his precinct captain again. Talk to some of those kids in the white T-shirts running around here with their pants off their ass. They'll let you know who Rivera is. They might even tell you a few things about yourself. I'd check around this office for storage lockers or loose floorboards. I think you have some automatic weapons hidden in here."

"You're kidding me." Ronson was starting to lose his composure.

"I wish I was," D said. "We'll talk soon, partner."

Shit, Damn, Motherfucker

D was in his apartment watching flying dunks and long-range threes on NBA.com while sipping on a green juice when his BlackBerry rang. It was Ray Ray's mother. Surely that meant bad news.

"What's going on, Janelle?"

"I wanted you to know that Ray Ray got picked up by the police."

"On what charge?"

"It was some of that stop-and-frisk shit," she said angrily. "They got him right in front of our building."

"Was Rivera involved?"

"That bastard's got his hands up in this for sure," she declared. "I know that."

"Ray Ray told me you two used to date."

"Like that's some of your business."

It sounded like D had crossed a line. He tried to jump back. "Okay, so how much bail money you need?"

"I got it covered. You ain't the only nigga I know." She wasn't going to let him off the hook. "You wanna help me, D?"

"Of course. I can come meet you right now."

"No, stay the fuck wherever you are. You can help me by never, ever getting my son involved in any of your shit again."

"I didn't ask him to follow Rivera, Janelle."

"That boy really loves you, D. You tell him something's wrong in your world and he tries to help. So you may not have wanted him to do anything, but he did it because of you."

"I hate to say this, but I think it's also about you and Rivera. Whatever happened between you two, your son didn't like it."

"Fuck you, D."

"Have him call when he gets out," he said, but wasn't sure she heard it before she clicked off.

He tried Ray Ray's phone but just left a message. Now restless and suddenly hungry, D got dressed and walked down Flatbush Avenue to a tiny Spanish food spot near Seventh Avenue. He was eating roasted chicken, red beans and rice, and sweet plantains when a lanky black kid in a flat cap and the falling-off-ass pants uniform of the borough entered and came his way. D grabbed his knife and was prepared to jam it into the young man's chest if he made a threatening move.

"D Hunter," he said warily, "you don't know me but we need to talk."

"Why do we need to do that?"

"Cause I know everything, yo," the kid said anxiously, "and I could use your help."

"That's a lot of words. Let's start with one at a time. What's *everything*?"

"Why Ice had guns in that bag at the fight club."

D realized it was the kid who Ice had dissed that night. The one who looked like his Mini-Me.

"Is that everything? Doesn't seem like it should affect my meal."

"I was there when that writer friend of yours got murked."

"What?"

"Skinny man with a gray beard. He caught it down in Soho. Can we talk now?"

"Okay. What's your name?"

"Freezy."

"Freezy? Not Lil' Freezy?"

"Can I sit down?"

"Go ahead, Freezy. My friend's murder: prove you were there."

He was clearly Ice's blood, though he had none of his father's intensity. There was a lot of weasel in his eyes, a nervous energy that suggested someone who lived for angles.

"Your friend, he fought hard. He actually got away from us—got around the corner. There was a gym there and these trainers came out, so we ran back to the car. And something you didn't know: it was the driver who jumped out the car, took my knife. His was the killing blow."

"What was the driver's name?"

"Alan Mayer." The name was actually Eric, but for D it was close enough.

"What did he look like?"

"White man. Older than you by a lot. Had a salt-and-pepper beard. Short. Army vibe. Dressed correct."

"How'd you meet him?"

"He had a lot of guns. You need some steel, he'd hook you up. Said he knew everyone in the rap game. Used to show us photos—Russell Simmons and people like that."

D gripped his fork tightly, contemplated jamming it down the kid's throat. "If you know that Dwayne Robinson was my friend and you helped kill him, why the fuck would I help you? Also, did Ice know you were gonna kill Dwayne?"

"You wanna go somewhere else to talk about this?"

"Here and now, Lil' Freezy. What did your father know?"

"He didn't know I was gonna do that. I didn't know either until we went to Manhattan. When I got in Mayer's car I thought we were just gonna buy some guns. He handed us a roll of bills and some knives and told us to stick that man. He told me he'd give me an Uzi. It was beautiful, yo. But I didn't know how to load it properly, and when I figured that shit out I saw that the white motherfucker sold me the wrong bullets."

"Nigga, I could kill you right now." His hand on the fork started shaking.

"I understand that, yo." Freezy stared at D's hand. "I get it. I just need some contacts and some help getting out of town."

"Why the fuck should I help you?"

"I know that Ice murked Mayer and I know you were there, and I could tie you to it. Right now it's a cold case. You feel me, yo? That said, I don't wanna do that. I really don't give a fuck about that white motherfucker and his bullshit. Truth is, I'm scared."

"Of Rivera?"

"Of him and all the shit that's going on. People treat me like I'm stupid, but I pay attention. Rivera and Mayer used to do business together. Well, really, Rivera taxed him for selling guns in Brownsville. After Mayer was murked, Rivera got Ice to take that shit over."

D's grip on the fork loosened. He was taking it in, wondering if he could trust the slimy young man before him.

"Ice told me he had the guns that day as a favor."

"It was for me."

"Yeah? Was he doing it for Rivera or for you?"

"For me, but he knew Rivera was involved. Thing is, Rivera is trying to cash out, get into buildings and shit. Real estate development, yo."

"A real gangsta."

"What?"

"Go on."

"So they were gonna get Ice vic'ed. Guess Rivera was through with him."

"How do you know all this?" D asked.

"I worked for the cop. I'm Ice's seed. I keep my ears open, yo."

"So you're a killer and a liar and you betray your father. I should trust *you*, yo?"

"I can tell you what Rivera has planned for you at Night's show at Betsy Head Park."

"Yeah?"

"Yeah, yo."

"So what do you want for that info?"

"Like I said, I'm getting out of Brooklyn. I'm gonna end up in jail or dead or some shit like that if I stay in this piece. I need a letter from you for my PO that I'm working for your company and will be traveling with the tour doing security for Night. When he calls, you can confirm that shit. I need to get out of town and I wanna do it clean."

D looked at Freezy like he was as crazy as his name. "Security? No way. I wouldn't hire you to do security if you gained fifty pounds and five inches. But you could be a roadie, a gofer. That could work."

"Whatever, yo. As long as you give me that paper and stand behind it, we're good."

"Me and you—we'll never be good," D said sourly.

"Okay. All right. Just hear what I have to say."

Reluctantly, D listened. Then he made his own plans.

THE ROOT

It was a beautiful day in Brownsville. The sun shone, the air was sweet. At Betsy Head Park families set up barbecue grills and there was much trash talk about who's homemade sauce had more flava. Women wearing platform sandals and their best weaves (that imported Indian hair was shining like new money) hovered near the temporary stage. The Ville's over-sixty residents came armed with fold-up chairs, creating an oasis of twentieth-century civility.

DJ D-Nice filled the air with old-school classics (Maze with Frankie Beverly on "Before I Let Go," the Blackbyrds' "Rockcreek Park," Earth, Wind & Fire's "That's the Way of the World," the Whispers' "Rock Steady," etc.) that were sure to make black folks smile, sip their sweet drinks (some laced with alcohol), and do the two-step. A white community-relations patrolwoman talked to little kids as they got their faces painted. There were whites scattered through the crowd, people undaunted by Brownsville's bloody reputation, resting on blankets, nibbling on goat cheese.

D stood on the side of the stage gazing out at the Betsy Head field and smiling. Here was a spirit of love. It's how you imagined your neighborhood could be: a place where everyone gathers and feels part of something.

D's cell buzzed. The text read, *5 minutes away.* He walked down the metal steps into the backstage area, which was basically three motor homes, a craft services table, and some deck chairs behind a few police barricades. A black Denali rolled onto the field and deposited Al and Night, along with Ride, who was on duty as Night's personal bodyguard.

"Okay," D said to Ride, "you know what to do."

"I do. You crazy, you know?"

"That was confirmed way back when. Whatever you do, stay with Night. That's your only job today, Ride. I can handle mine."

"Thank you, D."

"Do the job, impress Al, and good things can come out of this for you, including a trip to LA."

Night came over with Al. Ignoring the screams of some older women from behind the police barricades, Night said to D, "So this is your hood?"

"It's where I grew up. Don't know if I could really claim it now."

"Gonna give them a good show nevertheless. I like the hood love vibe out here."

Back in the trailer, Night, who was already in his stage gear, did yoga to limber up as Al spoke with tardy band members on his cell. Peering out the window, D could see Brownsville filling up the field and hear D-Nice spreading sonic love. Despite the low rumbling in his stomach, D was still smiling. It was going to be a good day for Brownsville. Of that fact he was sure. He wasn't so sure how it would work out for himself.

When there was a knock on the door, Ride opened it to find Cassidy Ronson and Faith Newman standing there.

D said, "They're good," and Ride bid them entry. The presence of the wannabe real estate mogul and the certifiable dot-com billionaire slightly transformed the room's relaxed mood to one of light wariness.

Faith kissed D's cheek and then moved quickly toward Night, who came out of a tree pose to hug her warmly.

"So," Night said, "you gonna sing with me today?"

172 of The Lost Treasures of R&B

"Really? I'd be honored."

"Just some background vocals. I wanna see if you can hang in the hood."

Faith giggled. While this ebony-and-ivory bonding was going on, a different version was being played out by D and Ronson.

"It's good to see you, D," Ronson said.

"Congrats on the show," D replied. "This is gonna be a great day in the hood and a good look for your company."

"Well, I wanted you to know that Detective Rivera is no longer in the employ of AKBK."

"So I've been told."

"You were right about him. In fact, it was worse than you said. His reputation is abysmal. Just letting him go is bringing a lot of good will our way."

"Good for you."

"D, would you like to help monetize that good will?"

"This is not the time or place for that conversation."

By now, a crowd of several thousand had gathered for the return of the soul messiah. A handful of folks wore T-shirts bearing the image of Night's butt from his famous video. Two very cute white girls sat on blankets holding up a *Bring on the Night* placard. In fact, since D had entered Night's trailer, the number of white faces in the crowd had increased, drawn by the rarity of the singer's free public appearance and the same pioneering spirit that made gentrification possible.

D glanced over at Faith, who was doting on Night, and he knew right then that even Brownsville, forsaken by the city for a century, could change. The realization hit him hard and reverberated through his soul. He'd listened to Ronson's pitch and the rhetoric about public planning and none of it had led him to believe that Brownsville could change.

But looking out at the crowd awaiting Night, D was suddenly con-vinced. It could happen. It *would* happen.

"Okay," Al said to Night, "let's do this."

D and Ride led Night and his band across the grass to the stage's metal stairs. As "One Nation under a Groove" flowed groovaliciously from the speakers, elders and hotties alike stood and cheered Night's arrival.

"Congrats," D said to Al as they both stood in the wings watching Night, his arms raised, bask in the love.

"Couldn't have done it without your help," Al said.

"Listen, Al, chances are I won't be here at the end of the show."

"What's up?"

"I'll get word to you."

"Huh?"

Without answering, D walked down the steps. Al watched him for a moment and then turned back toward the stage as Night began to sing. He wondered what was up with his friend, but this wasn't the time for curiosity. Night cut Al a look and they both smiled. It was finally gonna be all right.

During Night's third song, a bluesy tune called "Keep It Going," Rivera walked up very casually to D with a small smug smile. D knew that face wasn't good for him, and a moment later he felt the hard round edge of a silencer against his back. He didn't turn around. Whoever it was, it didn't matter—he was just a tool anyway.

"Come with me," Rivera said.

BAD HABITS

"There aren't a lot of things that really get me angry. I don't care if my wife fucks the mailman. I mean I haven't touched her in five, six years anyway, so if she can get it, God bless her, you know? I don't get mad when some hood rat tries to pull my cap. He's probably stupid and more likely to shoot his dick off or fuck up his finger in the recoil than hit me. So none of those normal-type things really irritate me. I mean I've been robbed before. No one likes to be robbed. I'm a damn cop so you know it's kinda embarrassing. But, end of the day, some fool gets a couple hundred dollars and some credit cards, it really is nothing when you look at your whole life. Besides, it always comes around. I usually see that guy again. But when someone steals your future? Well, that is very, very hard to take casually. You think I want to retire on a cop's pension? I had an exact strategy. An escape hatch where there was real money on the other side. Now I'm not quite sure where my future lies. That really, really bothers me."

D heard most of Detective Gerald Rivera's soliloquy, but parts of it were lost amid the punches being thrown and the reggaeton blasting in the room. He was tied to a chair with no blindfold, with a boxing mouth guard stuffed into his mouth and held in place by a bandanna tied around his head. His nose (at least the part of it that still worked) sniffed out mildew, gas, and industrial-strength cleaning fluid. This basement felt like the one in Canarsie where he'd watched Ice torture

Eric Mayer. He could have stopped that, but Mayer had killed Amina, a women he cared for, so he'd walked away.

Perhaps this ass-whipping was biblical retribution for that moral lapse. This basement wasn't in Canarsie though. It was in that same building off Livonia where Rivera sold guns to those kids. They were only a block or two from Betsy Head Park. Off in the distance D could hear Night's silky voice despite the painful ringing in his ears.

D was surprised at how articulate Rivera was even as the cop hit him—one, two, three times, left, right, left—in the stomach, left ear, right cheek. He'd expected broken English or dull cop speak. Instead, Rivera was as introspective as he was vengeful. *I guess he couldn't have set up all those brothers if he'd been a stereotype,* D thought.

But when Rivera picked up a baseball bat, D shuddered.

"Mr. D," the detective said, spittle flying into D's face. "I was the cleanup hitter on the Bayamón Angels this season. I led the East New York league with a .550 batting average. True, it was softball. The ball don't move that fast but it does move. Your big black head? That's just like a soft-tossed pitch." Rivera cocked the bat high, like Ichiro Suzuki in his prime. "The pitch is coming."

Then, from upstairs, came the sounds of a chair falling, a man groaning, and heavy feet. Rivera lowered his bat and listened.

"Teddy?" he called out. "Teddy, what's going on?" No reply. Rivera listened some more. "Teddy?" Again silence. The cop moved quickly then, setting the bat on the floor and pulling out a gun from behind his back. Through blurry eyes, D watched Rivera move cautiously toward the stairs, peering up toward the door.

D had noticed a back door to the basement. He had seen the small, dirty windows on either side of the room, though he knew they weren't wide enough for him to squeeze through.

"Teddy, if you hear me, say something!" From under his shirt Rivera pulled out his NYPD badge and kissed the shield like a cross. He slid a small-caliber gun from a holster on his right ankle and aimed at the top of the stairs. Now, guns in both hands, he took a deep breath and charged up, taking the steps two at a time. He banged through the door and D could hear his heavy feet moving quickly through the house.

D's eyes danced as his ears strained. He heard a new sound from behind him; the atmosphere in the room changed. Fresh air seemed to materialize from behind him with Night's voice somewhere in the distance. Then someone hit the basement floor. His body shook and the chair rattled when a dirty hand covered his mouth. Though his nose was likely broken, D could detect the aroma of menthol cigarettes and manure. A voice whispered, "Ssssssshuush." Rivera's heavy feet could be heard coming back toward the basement door and the hand left his face.

The fresh air disappeared. The window closed? D wasn't sure. He heard soft steps. Stealthy quick. Out of the corner of his right eye D saw movement as his apparent benefactor positioned himself under the staircase. D turned his head but his chair was too far forward for him to see anything but shadows.

The detective came down the stairs walking backward, his eyes (and guns) aimed at the doorway. Two gloved hands reached between the wood planks and yanked Rivera by his feet, sending him backward, sailing five feet down toward the basement floor. He unleashed a barrage of gunfire as he fell, shooting at the doorway, the staircase, the ceiling.

Rivera bounced off the floor, his grunt loud and pained. Then a single gunshot went *Blam!* and hit Rivera square in the forehead. The air was now heavy with gun smoke. A spent shell had landed against D's right arm and he jumped in the chair more in surprise than pain. He had not peed his pants since childhood but he felt a small bit of urine escape into his underwear.

"Yo, you alive?" The gritty familiar voice came from the top of the staircase.

From under the stairs a young, equally familiar voice said, "Yeah."

The older voice said, "Not you, fool."

"Oh yeah. D looks alive. Got his mouth stuffed up."

A pair of young hands suddenly worked at untying his bonds, while a man started coming down the stairs.

His mouth unstuffed, D's first words were "Why are you here?"

Ray Ray simply looked at him and continued working on his bonds.

"Because," Ice said as he stood over Rivera's prone body, "I needed him." He peered down at the cop, a glare of undisguised mirth spreading across his face.

On wobbly legs D walked over to where Ice stood. "You just made this boy an accessory to murder. That was not the agreement, Ice."

"I needed someone I could trust and right now he was the closest thing I could find," Ice replied softly. "This was a two-man job."

"I wanted to help," Ray Ray said to D's back.

D turned, grabbing the young man by the T-shirt. "You should not be here. In fact, you are not here and you never were. You understand me, you silly motherfucker?"

Ray Ray pulled out of D's grasp. "I saved your life, nigga."

"No," D said, "you ruined yours."

"You a dramatic motherfucker, aren't you, D?" Ice said as he rifled through Rivera's pockets. Satisfied there wasn't much of value there, he took the small gun out of Rivera's dead hand and replaced it with the Beretta he had just used. "Cover your ears, you two," he directed, and then squeezed two shots up the staircase toward the door. "That'll give those CSI guys plenty to play with. Okay, Ray Ray, you go back out that window. D, you head out the back door. Let's meet at the McDonald's in twenty minutes."

"I looked fucked up," D said.

"You *are* fucked up," Ice agreed, "but around here you'll fit right in."

D was back in that same McDonald's where he'd been meeting with Ride. Once Brownsville got gentrified, he figured, he'd do these sit-downs at a Starbucks. After finding an open table near the back window, D used napkins to stop the blood leaking from his nose and the ice from a Coke to nurse his various bruises. He had to get to a hospital, but before he made up the lies he'd need to pull that off, he needed some info.

Ray Ray came in and sat across from him. D was no longer angry, just disappointed.

"My moms got the bail money from Ice," Ray Ray related. "He told me what was up. That you were gonna get snatched up and that he was gonna follow you, but he needed another pair of eyes. I owed Rivera some payback for putting me back in the system. Plus, you have always looked out for me, D. He was gonna murk you."

D stared at him and shook his head. The kid's ghetto logic was sound, except that now he had a body on him and, though Ray Ray didn't know it yet, the weight of that dead cop's soul would hang on him for the rest of his days.

After ordering a Quarter Pounder, large fries, and a Coke, Ice joined D and Ray Ray. He smiled and said, "It all went according to plan."

Ice's angry son had, once D agreed to help him, shown him how to reach his father. It had taken a couple of days. It was all quite strange:

the son who betrayed Ice and then Rivera had facilitated this bloody day. D had learned long ago that the values of the street were where logic went to die. Perhaps that whole story about Ice and Rivera was just a setup.

Ultimately it didn't matter: Ice, with Ray Ray's help, had followed Rivera's car, figuring they'd take D someplace to inflict a little ultraviolence before dumping his body. Now it was Rivera's body that would have to be dealt with.

"What did you do with the other cop?" D asked.

"He's in a car trunk a couple blocks away. He's alive. Gonna have him left on the Grand Concourse with a bagful of guns and two bricks of cocaine. A solid citizen will phone in a report about the suspicious car. In a couple of days the NYPD will finally get around to checking it out. Not sure what his story will be to Internal Affairs, but it will be some crazy shit."

"What about Rivera?" Ray Ray asked.

"Who?"

"Oh," said Ray Ray.

"Yeah," said Ice.

D shifted in his seat, because he was uneasy and because his body was hurting in a dozen different places. Ice pushed a bottle of pills across the table. "Vicodin. Use them for two days. Then I'll take you to a clinic where you won't have to file any paperwork. You'll be in pain but it's the way to go. I've done it before."

D took the bottle, opened it quickly, popped two pills in his mouth, and washed them down with Coke. He stuffed four more in his pocket and pushed the bottle back over to Ice. "This is enough. Wouldn't like it to become a habit."

"Okay," Ice said, then reached back into his pocket, pulling out D's cell phone, wallet, and keys. "They had them upstairs. You got mad text messages."

Night, Al, and Faith were raving about the show and wondering where he was. They wanted to celebrate. He needed to lie down.

DIDN'T CHA KNOW

*A*mos Pilgrim said, "You look like shit."

It was three days after the concert and his torture/rescue from the bloody basement. D was sitting on a sofa in a room on the fortieth floor of the Trump Soho with a spectacular view of lower Manhattan and Brooklyn to his right. Pilgrim was facing him.

"I hear, and now I see, that you had a problem after Night's show in Brooklyn."

"It's handled," D said. He tried to look as poker-faced as he could with a broken nose.

"You handle things, no disputing that. You need help with the medical bills?"

"I have insurance."

"This isn't an offer of charity, D. You have been so helpful in helping get Night back on track. I think that young man is the missing link—not just in R&B, but in black culture. Having him back onstage and making music gives me hope for the future."

"I will be fine."

"You still hold me responsible for Dwayne and Amina's deaths?"

"Your stupidity started that whole mess that killed Dwayne." There was an awkward pause in the conversation.

"Okay," Amos finally said, "I accept that."

"What choice do you have but to accept the truth?"

"Can I show you something?" Pilgrim disappeared into a bedroom.

A woman's voice could be heard and then some laughter. He emerged with a leather case an attorney might use for legal briefs.

"You gonna sue me?"

"No. Make you some money."

The businessman sat down, unzipped the case, and removed three 45rpm records bearing the Motown logo. "I hear you've been looking for one of these."

D peered at the ancient vinyl and then picked up one of the records. A wry smile crossed his face. "Why three?"

"I got a copy as a gift from someone at Motown many years ago. Then someone else hipped me to how valuable it had become in the collector's market. You know how I feel about black history. We haven't agreed on a lot, but when I heard about you searching for it I grabbed the remaining two."

"That's all that's left?"

"That's all the copies I could find," Pilgrim said. "I been around this music business some fifty-odd years. I know a lot of people and this was all I could locate. So, you gonna make that British cracker happy?"

"Should I?"

"You took his money, D. You wouldn't wanna be a renigger." The two shared a laugh, which made D uncomfortable but he couldn't help it. "Here's what I suggest—if I may?"

"Go on," said D.

"I'm gonna keep mine. You give one to that cracker. You keep one for yourself."

"What would I do with it? Collecting isn't my thing."

"You are not a historian but you know the importance of legacy as much as the next man. You deserve a piece of it."

"This doesn't change anything that happened between us," D said.

"One day I hope you'll feel different. Until then, take these." Pilgrim slid two of the 45s back in the leather case and passed it to D. He offered his hand, which the big man looked at and then, reluctantly, shook.

SMILING FACES SOMETIMES

D was coming out of Prospect Park happily drenched in sweat after jogging a few miles in his Nets basketball shorts and a black T-shirt with the word *Night* written in script across the chest when he spotted Detective Robinson leaving the Brooklyn Public Library's main branch with a book under his arm. The detective was dressed casually in khaki pants and a sporty sky-blue short-sleeved shirt. He moved with the loose walk of a man way off duty.

For a moment D wondered if he should call out to the cop. He hadn't heard from them in a month. Let sleeping dogs lie. Just then Robinson turned, saw D, and smiled tightly.

"You a big reader, detective?"

"I have my favorites," Robinson said, and then sheepishly displayed a copy of Chester Himes's *The Real Cool Killers*.

"What's that about? Serial killers?"

"No, it's a novel. The writer was a brother who lived in Paris and wrote these books about crime in Harlem. Man had a great imagination. They make me laugh."

"No Kindle?"

"Nowadays," Robinson said, "we spend so much time looking at screens on my job that I really enjoy having paper in my hand. Hey, what happened to your face?"

D still had a lump on the right side of his forehead courtesy of Rivera. "A security issue while I was working for Night. You should see the other guy."

"We haven't found Ice yet." The social aspect of the conversation had just ended.

"I'm sure he'll turn up. He's a Brooklyn boy. Where's he gonna go?" D forced a laugh that Robinson didn't share.

"Yeah," the detective said, "he'll turn up. We'll find him in some cellar in East New York. His world is small. He'd be lost on the other side of the Brooklyn Bridge. You've probably noticed you haven't heard from us lately."

"I'm not annoyed that I ran into you, detective," D said as friendly as he could. "But your partner—I don't think he likes me."

"With all due respect, he read up on you and your family. The way they died. He just thinks you got a dirty gene. Some families do. We see it all the time. I don't always agree, but you never know. You aren't wrong until you're wrong." There was a silence now. D wasn't sure how to respond or if he even should.

"Struggle makes people do things, detective." With that, D started to walk away.

"That was a good thing you did," Robinson said to D's back. "The Night concert was good for Brownsville."

Smiling widely D said, "Thank you. People out there deserve all the positive stuff people around here take for granted."

"I agree. And hopefully we won't have to meet in an official capacity again."

"Hell yeah," D said.

The two shook hands and D crossed Eastern Parkway, feeling the detective's eyes on his back.

FISTFUL OF TEARS

D got off the 3 train at Rockaway Avenue, as he had thousands of times as a child, and walked across Livonia Avenue past the Tilden projects where he and his family had lived and perished in a New York City of legend and fear. He walked past 305, where his first girlfriend, a plump girl with big bangs named Brenda, had lived on the twelfth floor. He went by the parking lot where his brother Rashid had mastered the art of the stolen car and then the front "lawn," a patch of greenish dirt where he and his three brothers had played tackle football.

Behind 315 there was a community center where, back in the day, they'd held dance competitions, kids played board games, and Con Edison gave out free tickets to the deepest part of the old Yankee Stadium bleachers. D hadn't been inside the community center in years.

He wasn't sure how he'd feel when he got to the next corner. Repulsion, anger, sorrow, and regret were among the feelings that could have rippled through his consciousness causing him to drop to his knees in painful prayer as if this ghetto intersection was an altar to the sacrifices made in Hunter blood.

But when D finally placed his toes on the hard concrete slabs that constituted the northwest corner of Livonia and Mother Gaston, he felt nothing. He was as numb as if a dentist had administered novocaine to his whole black-clad body.

Then, creeping through that nothingness, came disappointment. After all this time, D couldn't believe that walking here hadn't evoked any passion in him, not even a moist eye. The tears had all drained out long ago, he guessed, in thousands of dreams and nightmares.

It wasn't the corner where his brothers died that mattered. His memories were the real site of his pain. This was just a corner under the elevated IRT line, no different than the other three corners here on Livonia and Mother Gaston where, it was quite likely, somebody else's brother or sister or father or mother had been gunned down, slashed, beaten, or gutted in the hard, sad decades since Brownsville had first been developed.

After so many troubled years, D had finally accepted that grief wasn't a location but a state of mind.

Interrupting these thoughts, Ray Ray called his name and walked up. "Why you wanna meet out here, yo?"

"This corner used to be important to me," D said, and then took the leather case from under his arm and had handed it to the young man. Ray Ray unzipped the case and pulled out the 45 single, looking strangely at this ancient technology.

"That's for you," D said.

"And what do I do with it?" Ray Ray asked.

"I dunno. You'll figure it out."

The End

The Lost Treasures Playlist:

"I've Got Dreams to Remember" by Otis Redding
"100 Yard Dash" by Raphael Saadiq
". . . Til the Cops Come Knockin'" by Maxwell
"Country Boy & City Girl" by County Boy and City Girl
"Inner City Blues" by Marvin Gaye
"That's the Way of the World" by Earth, Wind & Fire
"Ascension" by Maxwell
"I'll Always Love My Mama" by the Intruders
"You Got Me" by The Roots and Erykah Badu
"Pour It Up" by Rihanna
"Sumthin' Sumthin'"by Maxwell
"On & On" by Erykah Badu
"Live Like a King" by Night
"Fire We Make" by Alicia Keys and Maxwell
"Feenin'" by Jodeci
"A Change Is Gonna Come" by Sam Cooke
"Otherside of the Game" by Erykah Badu
"Tightrope" by Janelle Monáe
"Ask of You" by Raphael Saadiq
"I'm Coming Out" by Diana Ross
"Love Hangover" by Diana Ross
"Be Here" by Raphael Saadiq and D'Angelo
"Lonely Teardrops" by Jackie Wilson
"Gettin' in the Way" by Jill Scott
"Shit, Damn, Motherfucker" by D'Angelo
"The Root" by D'Angelo
"Bad Habits" by Maxwell
"Didn't Cha Know" by Erykah Badu
"Smiling Faces Sometimes" by the Undisputed Truth
"Fistful of Tears" by Maxwell

Also available from Akashic Books

THE PLOT AGAINST HIP HOP
a D Hunter Mystery by Nelson George
192 pages, trade paperback original, $15.95

Finalist for the 2012 NAACP Image Award in Literature

"Wickedly entertaining." —*Kirkus Reviews*

"A carefully plotted crime novel peopled by believable characters and real-life hip-hop personalities." —*Booklist*

"Part procedural murder mystery, part conspiracy-theory manifesto, Nelson George's *The Plot Against Hip Hop* reads like the PTSD fever dream of a renegade who's done several tours of duty in the trenches." —*Time Out New York*

"George's prose sparkles with an effortless humanity, bringing his characters to life in a way that seems true and beautiful." —*Shelf Awareness*

BROOKLYN NOIR
edited by Tim McLoughlin
320 pages, trade paperback original, $15.95

Featuring an original story by Nelson George

Brand-new stories by: Pete Hamill, Nelson George, Sidney Offit, Arthur Nersesian, Pearl Abraham, Neal Pollack, Ken Bruen, Ellen Miller, Maggie Estep, Kenji Jasper, Adam Mansbach, C.J. Sullivan, Chris Niles, Norman Kelley, Nicole Blackman, Tim McLoughlin, Thomas Morrissey, Lou Manfredo, Luciano Guerriero, and Robert Knightly.

Launched by the summer '04 award-winning best seller *Brooklyn Noir,* Akashic Books continues its groundbreaking series of original noir anthologies. Each book is comprised of all new stories, each one set in a distinct neighborhood or location within the respective city.

BLACK ORCHID BLUES
a novel by Persia Walker
320 pages, trade paperback original, $15.95

"Walker's exuberant third Harlem Renaissance mystery [is a] dark, sexy novel."
—*Publishers Weekly*

"[T]he tale is strengthened by plenty of period detail and a fine feel for both the gay underworld of Harlem in the 1920s and the sociopsychological dynamics of her characters. Best of all, [protagonist] Lanie has the makings of a strong series heroine. Walter Mosley fans, in particular, should look for more from this promising crime writer." —*Booklist*

"Put a Bessie Smith platter on the Victrola, and go with the flow on this mystery/romance/history mix."—*Library Journal*

BLACK LOTUS
a novella by K'wan
160 pages, trade paperback original, $11.95

"[A] heart-thumping thriller . . . K'wan does a masterful job of keeping readers on their toes right up to the very last page." —*Publishers Weekly*

"Fans expecting another thug-in-the-street story will be pleasantly surprised at this rough police procedural." —*Library Journal*

"K'wan steadily builds to a frantic, movie-worthy climax." —*Entertainment Weekly*

SWING
a novella by Miasha
160 pages, trade paperback original, $11.95

"Wise librarians will stock up and 'swing' this one over to erotica fans." —*Library Journal*

"A nicely paced thriller, balancing raunch with equally juicy interpersonal drama . . . a strong writer who is unmistakably in her element." —*Brooklyn Paper*

"A sleazy little gem of a book . . . Short, dirty, and a riveting page-turner . . . This is literature with teeth and claws." —Chicago Center for Literature and Photography

TALES OF THE OUT & THE GONE
stories by Amiri Baraka
202 pages, trade paperback original, $16.95

"Baraka is a poet down to his bones . . . [The stories] evoke a mood of revolutionary disorder, conjuring an alternative universe in which a dangerous African-American underground, or a dangerous literary underground—hell, any kind of an underground —still exists . . . In his prose as in his poetry, Baraka is at his best a lyrical prophet of despair who transfigures his contentious racial and political views into a transcendent, 'outtelligent' clarity." —*New York Times Book Review*, Editors' Choice